THE STATUE OF MOW

The Book Of Imaginari - Part Two

Richard Hayden

Copyright © 2021 Richard Hayden

This is a work of fiction. Names, characters, places, and incidents either are the product of the author's imagination or are used fictitiously. Any resemblance to actual persons, living or dead, events, or locales, is entirely coincidental.

All rights reserved. No part of this book may be reproduced or used in any manner (physical, digital, or broadcast) without written permission of the copyright owner except for the use of quotations in a book review. For more information, contact the copyright owner: richard.c.hayden@outlook.com

First paperback edition December 2021
First Kindle ebook edition December 2021

Paperback ISBN: 9798483126492

Book and cover design by Richard Hayden & Naomi Clare
Images by Richard Hayden

Twitter: @r_c_hayden
Instagram: @r_c_hayden
Facebook Page: Richard Hayden Author (@rchaydenauthor)

Dedication.

This is an Amazon Kindle Direct Publishing first edition of The Statue Of Mow, which is part two of three in The Book Of Imaginari.

The series would not exist without the love and support of my friends and family. To get to this point has been a rollercoaster of edits, changes, late nights, long days, updates, and more.

To those that have read draft after draft, I thank you. I would like to thank by name; Amy, Imelda, Jane, Janet, Jo, Josie, Lesley, Martyn, and Steve, though there are many more that have known about this project in some way, these people have contributed in no small way to this adventure.

Most of all though I would like to thank Naomi, without her inspiration, love, and support, I would not have got any further than chapter one. In many ways, Imaginari belongs to us both, and now I am sharing it with the world.

To everyone that has helped or has been aware of this project, however small, thank you.

I hope everyone enjoys reading it, as much as I have enjoyed writing it.

Richard.

CONTENTS

Title Page
Copyright
Dedication
Chapter 1   1
Chapter 2   12
Chapter 3   20
Chapter 4   28
Chapter 5   44
Chapter 6   53
Chapter 7   66
Chapter 8   79
Chapter 9   95
Chapter 10   111
Chapter 11   120
Chapter 12   132
Chapter 13   146
Chapter 14   159

Chapter 15	171
Chapter 16	182
About The Author	195

CHAPTER 1

Nearly two years had passed since the events on the hill changed Ellie's life forever. For the most part, life had returned to normal with a few minor changes and additions here and there. Ellie and Annabelle were in a relationship and going strong. Sophie and Simon were still seeing each other despite the distance between them. The biggest change though was in Ellie's approach to problems, situations, and life in general. The events that had unfolded previously were not positive at the time, but they showed Ellie how brave she could be. She would now stand up to the likes of Rochelle without question, this was easy compared to the Man. Even though everyone had supported what happened on the hill all that time ago, they all agreed to keep it between themselves. Secrets were not a good thing in general, but nothing good could come from sharing this one in particular. Ellie did not dream of the hill anymore, did not have nightmares or visits from spirits, in general she now led a normal teenage life. Weekdays at college, weekends working or hanging out with friends, the biggest decisions and pressures she was facing was what to do after college. The time since Ellie had faced off with the Man had passed them all by without any major incident. The scorched earth on top of the hill around the folly had healed and it was now lush and green once more. The stories of the cause had almost passed into legend and depending on who was telling the story at the time they varied a lot. Whilst walking along corridors at school or out and about in town Ellie had heard everything from "I heard it was a gang with blowtorches and flame throwers," to "It was just a solar flare bouncing off the moon." Both equally ridiculous, but to most still more believable than what had actually happened. Ellie had left school now and was at college, she was fortunate that Annabelle, Simon, and the others had all gone to the same college. This meant that even though they were in different lessons they could still see each other regularly and be the teenagers they wanted to be. At weekends Ellie also had a part time job at the local supermarket, she enjoyed this although the constant beep, beep, beep, of the till did get irritating sometimes. Annabelle also enjoyed Ellie's job, it meant she could go in and try to distract her in the aisles by making funny faces or just generally being sweet. Sweet was a word Ellie used to describe Annabelle regularly, she was quite besotted with her. At first there was a nervousness, Ellie was wary of the reaction from her parents and friends, but they were all incredibly supportive. Ellie often chastised herself for worrying so much – after all if they believed in her when taking on the Man Of Mow, then they would be supportive of her having a girlfriend.

It was Saturday, a sunny Saturday at that and Ellie finished work at four to be greeted by Annabelle outside holding an ice cream with a huge grin on her face.

"I assume there is one for me as well?" Ellie asked as she approached.

"Absolutely," Annabelle replied, her mouth full at the time. "Just over there in that ice cream van, go help yourself," she cheekily mused.

"Or I could just have some of yours," Ellie teased, and before Annabelle could react she had grabbed her arm and bitten a huge piece of the ice cream off the top.

"Hey!" Annabelle shouted, with very little anger or malice.

Ellie grinned, "What's yours is mine and what's mine is mine," she winked. "Come on, let's get home."

The two girls turned, linked arms, and headed across the car park to the bus stop. Annabelle was staying over at Ellie's this evening; the Fields family were having a barbecue with some friends from the village as well as Ellie's from school. Despite it being an eventful arrival and initial time in the village, they had really settled in and started to call it and the local area home. There were even going to be some ex-council members there this evening. Kevin and Hannah had become close friends to Ellie's parents Katherine and Nicholas. The council had kept to their word and had disbanded after what happened by the folly. A little over a year after the incident Douglas and Beryl had passed away and for the first time a council member house had been sold in the normal way without any interference. The families in them had been left to settle in. Life was good in Mow Cop. Ellie and Annabelle boarded the bus and took their seats, much to Annabelle's frustration they shared the ice cream until it was all gone. Not long after, they arrived at their stop to get off. It was just around the corner from Ellie's home but before they walked back Ellie paused and looked up at the folly. There it was, proud as ever against the blue-sky background and looming over all that lay before it.

"Do you ever look and wonder?" Ellie asked softly.

Annabelle moved beside her and followed her eyes up the hill, "Wonder about what?" she asked, leaning her head on Ellie's shoulder.

"Just, about what happened. What it would have looked like from all the way down here? Or what would have happened if I had gotten it wrong?" She turned to face Annabelle. "It's all in the past and I don't really think about it much, but I do wonder every now and then, know what I mean?"

Annabelle lifted Ellie's hair out of her face, "The only thing I wonder is how dull my world was before you came along. You're amazing Eleanor Fields, my everything," she kissed her.

Ellie smiled, she loved it when Annabelle did that, made her go all warm and fuzzy. "So, you were duller before me? Wow! Didn't know that was possible," Ellie teased.

With that, the two smiled at each other turned and walked to Ellie's house to get ready for the evening's festivities.

Getting ready was always an event, especially for Ellie and Annabelle. They did not take ages, but always made sure they got the others opinion on outfits before emerging to attend the event in question. On this occasion, a summer barbecue, both had opted for outfits that would allow them to relax and enjoy the evening sun. By the time they were back downstairs, Nicholas and Katherine had finished preparing the salads, so all that was left to do was to cook the meat – this would be done after guests had arrived and settled though.

"Hey girls," Nicholas called as they entered the kitchen. "Looking lovely as always I see."

"Thanks dad," Ellie replied, giving a little twirl, "We wanted to make an effort as a couple." She grinned and looked at Annabelle. Together they pulled in close and posed for Ellie's parents.

"What are you like?" Katherine interjected. "Now could you go and do the drinks bucket please? There are beers, wines, cokes, and ice in the garage. They all need to go in the big bin outside and topped up with water to keep cool. Can you manage that in between cuddles and poses?"

She was teasing, Ellie and Annabelle knew this, but they also knew that there was a serious request in there as well, so they immediately left the room to do as she had asked.

A little while later, the party was in full swing. Ellie and Annabelle had been joined by Simon who was waxing lyrical about his recent visit to London to see Sophie. She had been invited too but was on holiday with her parents so could not be there.

"It's so hard being in a long-distance relationship," Simon bemoaned. "I mean, we can't just spontaneously do anything, know what I mean?"

"I understand," Annabelle agreed, "but you do have some advantages, Simon."

He raised an eyebrow, "Like what?"

"Yes Annabelle," Ellie chimed in, "What exactly are the benefits compared to what we have?" She had turned to face Annabelle now.

Ellie was teasing, but wanted to string Annabelle along a little, after all, she would do the same if it had been the other way around.

Flushing slightly, Annabelle responded, "Ok, before anyone gets carried away or any ideas, all I meant was they spend more time making the most of the time they have. None of their time together is wasted."

"Wasted? We waste time, do we?" Ellie asked, still teasing but also a little hurt at the same time.

"No darling, we don't waste time, I simply meant that when they get together there is always a reason. We do that too, but we can also get on each other's nerves a little. Remember a few weeks ago?"

Ellie went to respond, but then bit her lip instead. They had not had a fight as such, but they had come to realise they were spending a lot of time together, so had agreed to make time for family and other friends.

"See," Annabelle replied confidently. "I didn't mean anything by it, honest." She pulled Ellie into a hug and kissed her on the cheek, "You're special to me, more than you will ever know. Just don't annoy me too much is all."

Ellie smiled, "You're right. She's right Simon, too much of a good thing and all that."

"Easy for you both to say whilst you're in each other's arms though isn't it," he huffed and walked off to find something to eat.

The fact is everyone was very content with the way their world was. They had all sailed through the last few terms at school, some had part time jobs but most importantly, they had each other. Through the evening Ellie spoke to almost everybody at the party, she loved socialising but also found it exhausting at times. She spoke to Annabelle's parents Jack and Audrey, Kevin and Hannah too. All of whom were very fond of Ellie for different reasons. Kevin and Hannah because they knew what she had done, Jack and Audrey because they could see how happy she made Annabelle. There were quite a few people there from Nick's and Katherine's workplaces, people that Ellie knew by name and would make pleasant conversation with but not enough to chat with for hours on end. Those that knew what Ellie had done had said thank you and well done a million times over. Ellie had always welcomed it graciously and said thank you for their support.

She did not mind the positive attention. She did not want thanks or lots of people remembering and commenting but knowing she had made a difference meant the world to her. Ellie was ok with that.

Much later, after everyone had eaten their fill of burgers and sausages the party goers began to say their goodbyes. It did not take long for it to just be Nicholas, Katherine, Jack, and Audrey, with Ellie and Annabelle. Simon had wanted to stay, but he and his mother had an early start as they were going away the next morning.

"This really is unusual isn't it?" Jack asked of Nicholas, he was referring to the stone standing in the garden.

Ellie and Annabelle looked at each other.

"What is it, a bird Table?"

"In all honesty, Jack. We have no idea," Nicholas replied, a knowing nod towards his daughter as he did so. "All we know is it goes down deep, very deep. We tried to move it when we first moved in, was having none of it. So, Katherine made it into a feature for that flower bed."

"Well it certainly is that," Audrey replied, she too had been fascinated by the stone. "It's so weird to the touch isn't it?"

They all nodded in agreement.

"Would anyone like another drink?" Katherine called from the kitchen door.

"Americano please," Audrey replied.

"Nothing for me," Jack stated.

"I'm fine thanks," Annabelle added.

Ellie had concluded that Annabelle and Jack were as close as she was to her dad.

Ellie stood, "I'll come and give you a hand mum," she called, moved into the kitchen, and began helping with drinks.

Katherine did the coffee for herself and Audrey, Ellie made a lemonade for herself and a vodka and lemonade for her dad.

"This really is home now isn't it, mum?" Ellie commented, turning to face Katherine. "We have really settled in and whilst I do miss some of the things from London, I'm really happy here."

Katherine considered this, "I'm glad you feel that way Ellie, although I'm sure the majority of that is to do with the young lady outside with dark hair?"

There was a loving smirk on Katherine's face at this.

Ellie flushed a light shade of pink, "Well yes, she helps a lot, but I didn't just mean that. I mean I feel like we have lived here forever, like we never lived in London. It's home."

She smiled at her mother, who returned the same smile.

"I feel the same way, Ellie. Now let's take these drinks out before these go cold and those get warm."

A little while later, Jack and Audrey had left and the Fields family, plus Annabelle, were all getting ready for bed. Annabelle was sleeping in Ellie's room on the pull-out bed, this was a situation that had happened a lot recently. Ellie had stayed at Annabelle's before, but there was more room here. Ellie had got ready first and was lying on her front, chin resting on her arms, so she could look up and smile at Annabelle as she entered the room from the bathroom.

"What?" Annabelle asked, a quizzical look on her face.

"Nothing, just reminding myself how beautiful you are and how I now feel that this place is my real home."

Annabelle blushed, and headed over to sit next to Ellie, pulling her blonde hair out of her face as she did so. "I'm glad you feel at home because you're never leaving now! Mwah ha ha ha ha," Annabelle teased in a mock booming voice.

She also tickled Ellie a little as she did so, the pair knew exactly how to push each others buttons in the right way and were without question, a team. When they had calmed down, and Annabelle was in her pull-out bed, Ellie leaned over the end of the bed and asked, "When did you know you wanted to be with me?"

Annabelle looked up, "What do you mean?"

"Well, I remember being at the Halloween party at school years ago, and you said that you made it known to people that you wanted to be with them. When did you decide you wanted to be with me?"

Annabelle smiled, "Ellie, sweet innocent Ellie. There wasn't a single moment, I guess you just wore me down bit by bit with your charm and wit," she smirked.

"I'm serious," Ellie replied, throwing a pillow at Annabelle in frustration.

"Well violence will certainly make me talk," Annabelle chuckled. "Look, I can't say it was love at first sight, I'm not sure it was. Of course, I saw your gorgeous smile and eyes the moment we met. But as I got to know you, the real you, the way you stood up to everyone, held your own, was brave, and willing to sacrifice everything. That's when I knew."

Ellie smiled at this, "So, on the hill then?"

Annabelle grinned, "If that's what you want to believe, then that's what happened." She lay back down on her pillow. "The simple fact though," she continued with her eyes closed, "is I fell for you because you're awesome, Ellie, don't ever forget that."

Ellie, blushing, grinned widely. "Thanks Annabelle, you're awesome too. So awesome, I may start calling you Bella for short."

"You can, but you will only be able to do it once," came the stern reply.

"Night, Annabelle," Ellie retorted, emphasising the full pronunciation of her name.

Annabelle mimicked the same tone, "Night, Eleanor."

With that the two girls went to sleep.

A few days later, Ellie was sat at home looking out of her round window. It was a pleasant view. The summer had been kind and the clear blue sky contrasted perfectly with the green of the grass and trees. Unlike at the weekend, there was a gentle breeze that took the edge off the suns heat. She had spent more than enough time sat in it of late to know that it was a cooler day, but just as sunny and glorious to be in. Annabelle was working, her parents were at work, she had the house and indeed the day to herself. Until later that was, she was meeting Annabelle after work, they were going to go bowling. Being a competitive pair, they kept score and so far, Annabelle was winning three - one in terms of games. Ellie was determined to change this tonight. She looked at the clock, twelve thirty, she had hours to kill yet and very little to do. She had already done the housework that she had promised her mother she would do. After a little deliberation, Ellie decided to go for a walk, she tied her hair up in a ponytail, grabbed some water, and headed out of the door. She was right, it was hot, and after a short distance she was already working up a sweat. Fortunately, she had the foresight to only wear light clothing. This meant she would need to change before tonight but that was ok, there was lots of time before then. She walked casually and slowly up the hill, following the route she had taken the very first time she had gone up the hill in Mow Cop. It was still a tough walk, but after living in the village for a time she knew better how to pace herself when walking up the hill. After a short while she had made it to the folly, the location of her showdown with the Man years before. The folly itself had not changed as it was still a ruin, but Ellie knew the truth now as to what the building actually was and what it meant to the existence of the world. She looked up at it, standing above the village and surrounding area. Turning, she made her way to the rockier area at the top of the hill, the view up here was always breathtaking, and Ellie sat and soaked it all in. It was not too far from here that she had first met Simon, he had charmed his way into her life with a bag of sweets and a smile. Ellie grinned to herself, she did love her friends. She decided to retrace the steps of that first visit up the hill, so she stood and moved over to the rock she had been lying on when he had popped up in her sunlight. She turned to take in the view she had that day, it was as gorgeous as she remembered it.

What was next? Ellie pondered to herself. Then she remembered he had started talking about the Man Of Mow and had told her of the rocks that looked like him round the back of the hill. So, off she went. It was a short walk, across the top of the folly hilltop, through some farmer's fields and then round to the left. This was one of Ellie's favourite places, as on one side there was Staffordshire, and the other Cheshire. Ellie had brought Annabelle up here on bonfire night, "Don't need to buy fireworks, just watch everyone else's for miles around you," she had commented at the time. Continuing, she walked along a stone path. The folly was not visible from here due to the trees and the shape of the hill, but she knew exactly where she was and where she was going. Before long, she had arrived at the rock formation. The rocks that the locals called the Man Of Mow. Ellie recalled how Simon had to hold her head in a certain position so that she could see the figure. It did need a certain angle, but she could find it quite easily now. She stared at the rocks, for a moment, everything else seemed to disappear around her, as if it was just her and the rock face. She shook her head to clear the mind lock that seemed to be happening to her right now. She took a drink of water, It is just rocks, she told herself. Indeed, in her confrontations with the Man, he had never mentioned this area or rock face, it clearly was just a pile of rocks. Ellie could not help the feeling of being watched though. She turned around in a full circle, nobody. She decided it was probably the nervousness as to the wording on the council issued signage around the rock face. '*Keep off the rocks*,' and '*Do not enter*,' were the two that Ellie could see on the fence from where she was. There was something else though, something that felt off. Ellie decided to investigate, taking a few steps forward she lifted herself over the small wooden fence and approached the rock face. The feeling was different here, even though it was only a small fence she felt cut off from the rest of the world. She felt silly for doing so, but she turned to check the world was still there, it was, so she carried on. As Ellie approached the rock face she could hear a buzzing, a hum, as if there was an electric current flowing nearby. As far as she was aware there was no such thing. Ellie tilted her head to try and focus on the sound to work out where it was coming from. After listening for several seconds, she determined that it was coming from the rocks themselves. Rocks don't hum, Ellie thought to herself, there was no doubt it was coming from them though. She was close now, close to one of the stones that made up the statue of the Man Of Mow. From here though it did just look like a pile of rocks. She reached out her hand to touch the surface of the rock. As her skin got closer to the surface the hum got louder and she could feel an invisible force pushing back against her hand. She pushed on. Then, just before her skin made contact with the rock there was a loud bang. Ellie's hand was now sucked onto the rock and held fast, the same way a magnet locks onto the surface. She could not release it, could not free her hand from the surprisingly warm stone. She looked around to call for help, but there was nobody there. More specifically, there was nothing there. The view, the fence, the grass, and the trees, all of it had gone. It had been replaced by a purple smoke, a haze that flowed around her the way that steam rises above a hot cup of tea. The only thing left was the rock her hand was stuck to, and herself. Ellie tried to free her hand, pushing against the rock with her other hand, and then one foot. Nothing. It would not move.

She screamed out in frustration, "What the heck is happening now?"

Ellie had not been expecting a reply, but she got one none the less.

"Well, well, well. This is a nice surprise," a soft, male voice spoke. "How nice to see you again, Eleanor Fields."

CHAPTER 2

Ellie closed her eyes and froze. She knew that voice, she did not need to ask or see to know who was speaking to her.

"Is this your next ploy? Superglue on a rock?" she asked confidently. Not knowing what was going to happen next, Ellie did not know how to act but she knew she needed to act with confidence.

"My apologies, no, not superglue as you say but I can release you now, for you cannot go anywhere at the moment anyway."

His voice was calm, and almost soothing, but made Ellie's blood begin to boil with rage. She knew she needed to stay calm though, and not give him the satisfaction of an immediate reaction. In an instant the rock disappeared, and Ellie's hand was free once more. She examined her palm, no pain but a faint mark where the stone had been, as if her own palm print had another layer to it that was now visible. If she was not in her current predicament, she would have thought it was a henna tattoo from a holiday abroad somewhere. She lowered her hand and turned. Nothing. Or rather, just purple haze all around.

"So, where are we this time?" she asked, deciding to go on the offensive a little.

There was a chuckle, "This time Eleanor, I have the upper hand. This time, we are going to finish this in a way that you cannot even begin to comprehend."

"Finish this? Didn't we already do that, you lost I won, big bolts of light in the sky and so on."

Another chuckle, "Yes, that did happen. The last two years have given me time to reflect on that moment and see if there was a way to recalculate the events. In here I do lose all but two things."

There was a pause.

Ellie nodded forwards, "Well, want to share or shall I just leave now?"

"Oh, I will share, and to be clear, you will not be leaving, at least, not yet. The two things that I could never lose are time and my mind. Put them together and I can create plans and schemes of great complexity and power to achieve my goal. The goal of absorbing the power from your world into my own, into Imaginari."

"Right, so this is another power play then is it?"

"You have no idea what I am capable of and what is going to happen next."

"Please share, I want to know how you are planning on allowing Imaginari to thrive," Ellie replied. She was trying to stay calm and in control, but it was getting to be challenging. Had he really come up with another way to achieve his goal?

"All in good time, but first, I want to talk about time. Do you know how time works Eleanor? Real time?"

Ellie considered this, deciding for the sarcastic approach she eventually replied, "You mean like what time I had breakfast? Or when I am meeting Annabelle? Yeah, I know that time really well."

More chuckles, "Eleanor, always the comedian, but that will not help you now. This is how time really works."

As he finished, a blue line appeared in front of Ellie, floating around head height. It appeared to be moving like a river from her left to the right.

"Time is a flow, and in most ways a constant, it cannot be tampered with or changed."

Then lots of yellow lines appeared, twisting and wrapping themselves around the blue line, like a snake around its prey. Some were small circles, others were big, long sweeping curves from left to right.

"These are the spirit energy flows; you remember those I am sure. Everything in both your world and mine has an energy flow. It cannot be lost. It just gets replaced or moved on to a different point to be used by another being in a different way."

"Reincarnation?" Ellie asked, more out of wanting to say something than anything else.

"Yes, your people have been known to call it that. A way for people to deal with death I suppose. But it is far deeper than that."

The blue line got wider now and moved to the right allowing Ellie to see the left-hand side of the line in detail. She looked closely at the wisps now flowing in front of her, they were moving steadily, and if she looked closely she could see the formations of shapes, people even.

"Look closer," he instructed.

Ellie did so, although more out of general curiosity than following his orders. She looked deeper, further into the blue mist as it flowed past her eyes. Two shapes, two people, definitely people. Ellie could make out their body shapes now, arms, legs and everything in between. Though she could not place any specific details to them, they seemed to be generic people shapes.

"Do you see it yet?" he asked.

Ellie could hear the joy in his voice now, he was gloating.

"What exactly am I meant to be seeing?" she asked incredulously.

He chuckled once more, "Eleanor Fields you disappoint me. I would have expected you to recognise your own parents even if this image is from around eighteen years ago."

Ellie took a sharp intake of breath, the realisation hitting her like a hammer. The picture was in full focus now, she was looking at her parents holding a baby. They looked younger and she certainly had not recognised them right away, but it was undoubtedly them. Ellie concluded that the baby must be her.

"Is that me?" she asked, nerves well and truly setting in now.

"Very good, very good," came the soft, calm reply. "This is not long after you were born, Eleanor. This is your personal timeline."

The blue pulsated at this, as if to highlight the point to her.

"So, if this is me, what are all the other yellow swishes? Have I held that much energy all this time?"

"Now you are starting to understand, the yellow swishes as you call them are where you have come into contact with the energy flow to or from our world. It has always been a part of you, always will be."

"Ok, still not seeing a plan here," Ellie had got some fight back in her now, even though very little had been revealed, she did not like the idea of her family being impacted and involved.

"My child, you will soon understand all of it, but first, I want to explain how time can and cannot be manipulated."

"Manipulated? You're going to go back in time and kill me or something?" Ellie turned in a full circle, she wanted him to show himself so that she could vent some of her anger directly at him rather than at nothing.

"Sadly, that cannot happen. If I did that, then everything in your timeline would be removed, and as much as you are annoyingly headstrong, some of the things you have done have been more than useful."

"What then?" Ellie asked, as much confusion as fear in her voice now.

"I do not need to remove you from your timeline, I just need to make a subtle change to it. Right here," as he finished this the blue line moved a little further along. "This moment Eleanor, before you were born is where the life energy that flows through you even to this day was given to you. This is where I will carry out my scheme."

"Show yourself," Ellie shouted, "Be a brave man and show yourself to me rather than hiding in wisps of purple smoke."

Nothing. Ellie looked around her, still nothing. Then out of nowhere four strands of golden light lashed themselves around each of her wrists and ankles. They immediately pulled tight, stretching Ellie on the spot into a star shape so she could not move. Then, without warning and with a complete shock factor, the hollow face of the Man Of Mow appeared inches from Ellie's. It was unchanged from their last meeting, but the sheer surprise of it and the fact that she could not move or defend herself terrified Ellie.

"Is this where you wanted me, Eleanor? So, you can see me, look into my eyes and know your enemy has bested you?" he gloated.

Ellie was a little speechless at this, but soon recovered herself, "All you've done is tell me a story and shown me a picture, not seen anything worrying yet."

It was braver than she actually felt, here and now she knew she was powerless to get away from him.

"All I need to do, is make a simple change, everything up to now will remain as it was, and I am not changing the past. But, come the first winter moon, the same one when we faced off on the hill nearly two years ago, the outcome will be very different. This one change will alter the way your whole life has been played out to this very point. All I need is this."

He reached out a bony, ghost like, frail hand towards Ellie's head, Ellie braced herself for pain but there was none. As his hand reached her forehead and passed through it, it only felt a little cold. The sort of feeling you got when leaning into a fridge on a warm day. He moved his hand a little whilst it was still inside Ellie's head. Then as he pulled away to remove it, he was pulling something. It looked as if he had collected it from inside Ellie's mind. He floated a little further away from her and raised the hand that was holding the yellow wisps of light. His hand was now level with Ellie's head a short distance in front of her.

"This Eleanor, is you," he raised his voice as he reached the end of the sentence, as he did so the yellow mist he had been holding took shape and form, it grew arms, legs, and a head. It became a mirror image of Ellie. The only difference was that it was made of yellow light, but it was in the exact same position as she was, looking straight back at her.

"You see," the Man gloated as he moved to the side, meaning Ellie could see him clearly once more. "This is your life force. This is the spirit that makes you, you. This is one of many that could have been given to you on that day before you were born."

"Ok, still not following," Ellie butted in, she was getting very nervous about the situation now.

"All I am going to do, is make a subtle change, a tweak as it were, that will change two things about you that will play into my hands. I will have to wait, I must be patient, but as I say time is something I have."

"I will never do what you want me to do, no matter what you change or try I will always fight you."

"I have no doubt, in fact, I'm counting on it. But for now, let's just make a change shall we."

He raised his right hand once more, and this time quickly lowered it again slicing through the yellow ghost like figure floating opposite Ellie. As he did so, she felt a pain so deep and strong it was unlike anything she had experienced before. It felt like a migraine but across her entire body all at once. She screamed in agony, the feeling shot from her head and down her spine as if she was being split in two.

"The pain is deserved but will pass child," he gloated over her.

Ellie closed her eyes tight, scrunching them shut through the pain. Moments later, just as she felt like it was reaching an unbearable level, the pain stopped. It passed as quickly as it had arrived. Ellie opened her eyes. She was still held fast by the wrists and ankles, unable to move, but the floating figure in front of her had become two floating figures. He had split it in half, and in doing so each had formed into a replica and filled out so that Ellie was now staring at two yellow floating ghosts of herself.

"What does that do?" Ellie said, although she was struggling for breath and energy now, she felt as though she had been winded and could not breathe properly.

"That my child, is called the splice. I have pulled your spirit energy from you and split it in two. As much as I would like to watch you suffer as you are, you must have one of these back. For without it, you will die."

Ellie looked up at this, she had not noticed that her head had started to drop, the energy was leaving her body now and was only held up by the bonds to her wrists. "What do you mean?" her voice was faint, fading to a whisper.

"I mean that without this energy flow your body will crumble, and I do not want you to die. Not yet anyway."

The Man moved to one of the floating yellow ghosts of Ellie, pinched it by the head and flung it at her. It moved through the air like a cloud, the moment it made contact with Ellie's chest she felt a surge of energy and life flow through her. Immediately, she felt more awake and alert although still in the same predicament.

"Better now?" he asked, a faint sound of amusement in his voice.

He did not have lips as such, but Ellie knew if he did they would be curled into a cruel smile about now.

"Where was I? Ah yes," he moved to the remaining floating ghost of Ellie and stood by its elbow.

Ellie fought against her bonds, but they would not slacken off, she was held tight.

"I would save your strength if I were you, you will not break out of those," he had his back to her now, between her and the yellow spirit of Ellie. "All I have to do is this," he reached out both hands, and as far as Ellie could see all he did was put them inside the yellow spirit and swap his arms over, as if dealing cards or moving some cups around.

The ghost glowed a bright yellow, so much so it became impossible to see what it was other than it was a glowing yellow human shape in front of her. When the light faded, the Man moved to one side and Ellie was no longer face to face with herself, but face to face with someone who looked a little like her. The sort of differences that people comment on between siblings.

"Who is that?" she asked, fear very much in her voice now.

"That, Eleanor, is who you could have been. That is who is going to help me and destroy you, and your world, once and for all."

He grabbed the spirit by the head in the same way he had grabbed the one that he threw back into Ellie. This time though, he threw it into the blue timeline. Ellie had forgotten it was there until this point, as it hit at the moment before Ellie's birth there was a blinding white light. It burst out of the timeline like a firework, sending shockwaves and ripples all the way along its length.

Ellie had been expecting to feel something at this point, but there was nothing. "Am I supposed to still be here?" she asked, her full sarcastic range now in play.

"Oh yes, I did not kill you today Eleanor. All I did was change your world to be more, shall we say, to my liking. After our previous encounter I could not possibly kill you so kindly and quickly. I want you to suffer as I have suffered. I want you to feel helpless as your world crumbles around you. But first, I think you are owed an explanation as to where you actually are, I think that is fair."

"I thought we were in your prison space again? It looks the same."

"Yes, it does, however that is not where we are. You entered by touching a rock on the rock pile yes? The one the locals call the Statue Of Mow?"

"You should know, but yes."

"Well, this is part of the realm we saw before, but a different space I was able to work my way into. You see, this is a powerful place, a place that held power before the folly was built."

He waved his hands, in moments, the purple smoke faded away revealing a clean empty hilltop. The bonds holding Ellie were also released and she dropped to her knees, her arms by her sides exhausted. She looked around. There was a hilltop but no fences or signs. There was green grass all around and trees blowing in the wind. To one side there was an alcove cut into the side of the hill, next to it a large stone that looked a lot like the one she had touched on the hilltop that started this little escapade.

"Where is this?" Ellie asked. "When is this?" she added, she was more breathless than she had first realised at this point.

There was a chuckle, "This, Eleanor, is a time before the folly was built. A time before the first council even began to carry out my scheme. This is the home of Abijah."

CHAPTER 3

"You've sent me back in time?" Ellie asked, mustering as much energy as she possibly could to sound strong.

"Sort of, but not quite," the Man replied, he was now floating beside Ellie, facing the same way she was.

The way they were facing was towards what can only be described as a hole in the hilltop. It looked like an alcove cut into the side of the hill. There was a place where someone had apparently been sleeping, the flattened leaves and pile of rocks for a pillow gave that away. There were markings on the wall as well, they could be considered cave drawings except this was not a cave. Ellie could not quite make out what it was. A sort of half-way house between a cave and little alcove in the side of a hill that somebody, apparently Abijah, was using for a home. Ellie took a step closer, as she did so the Man spoke once more.

"We are simply exploring a recreation of another time; we cannot interact with what we see in the same way they cannot react to us. As I say, this is the home of Abijah, or at least it will be. For now, it is just an area where I chose to visit him way back before the folly, he became obsessed and started to rest, visit, and sleep here more often. Eventually he built himself a hut here."

"So, why are you showing me this? If this is just an area where a crazy guy slept a million years ago, why show me?" Ellie was getting frustrated now, but she needed him to talk, that was the only way she was going to figure out what to do next.

"Crazy man?" came the reply, "How can you say he was crazy? Everything he spoke of and planned for came true did it not?

The folly I designed with him, for him, worked in a fashion. The villagers here certainly believed and followed his lead." There was a tone to his voice that suggested he was mocking her.

"Ok, so he wasn't crazy, but that was only because you made him do what you wanted him to do. It became true because you then did what you wanted, which is what you told him to do." Ellie paused, she had confused herself a little but after a few seconds recovered, and turned to face the Man. "What I mean is, the only reason it all becomes true, is because you made it so. He was just a normal guy until you came along and filled his head."

Nothing.

"Silent treatment now is it?" Ellie asked, indignantly. "Nothing else to say..." but she was cut off.

As she was speaking a figure moved through the Man directly towards her. Dark hair, wrinkled face with soft brown eyes. He walked with a slow confidence directly towards Ellie, she instinctively moved to one side out of the direction he was travelling. As he passed, Ellie took note of his appearance. He was a little taller than she was, his simple clothing hid his figure and body shape, but he did not look unfit to her. He was carrying a small box in his hands, out in front of him as if it was very delicate. When he reached the alcove, Ellie moved closer to look at what he was doing. He had sat down legs crossed with the box in front of him. Placing his hands on his knees he closed his eyes and began to sway gently from side to side. Ellie noticed his lips were moving, but the sound was so quiet she could not quite make it out.

"What is he doing?" she asked.

"Praying. Chanting. Essentially, he believes he is summoning me. As you say, he did not really possess any power I simply bent his mind to my will. Tonight, will be the second time he has seen me, the first time I gave him the words to repeat over and over."

Ellie snapped her head around to face him, "That's cruel," she exclaimed.

"Maybe, but for me it was a way of testing his will and belief. Remember child, this is a time when what is strange is seen as something to be feared. He feared me, so he did what I asked."

"Still cruel," Ellie retorted, turning back to look at Abijah. "So, is he just chanting until you return to him? How long is that going to be?"

"I did not return until this evening," the Man replied. "But we can get there quicker."

For a moment Ellie had forgotten that they were in a recreation, he raised his arms and with a flick of his wrist, the surroundings changed. They were in the same place, as indeed was Abijah, but it was now night and the sky was clear and full of stars. Ellie looked around, nothing had changed, and indeed Abijah had not moved, lit a fire, or anything. He was still there apparently repeating the same words over and over it seemed.

"What did you make him repeat?" she asked, it did not seem that relevant necessarily, but she felt she needed to know.

"I made him repeat a five line verse," came the reply. Then, he started to speak in a tune compared to his usual soft tones.

"Man 'O Mow, Come show us how.
Protect us, save us, lead us.
Man 'O Mow, I am yours to command.
Protector of the then, the will be, and the now.
We will live by your hand, Man 'O Mow."

Ellie stared at Abijah, now that she had heard the Man speak the words she was able to line his lips up to them and see that he was indeed in a trance like state. "You made him say that, over and over until you returned to him? Making him think that he was summoning you like some kind of god?"

"Correct. Truthfully I am already here, just over there," he pointed to his right.

Ellie turned to look, and true enough there was the ghostly representation of the Man in the recreation. He was floating a short distance away, watching.

"You knew he wouldn't open his eyes to look at you, didn't you? You knew you could have been right in front of him and he would never have known!" Ellie's anger was increasing now, she could feel the pressure building inside her.

"Yes, I knew he would not stop until I announced myself. It made it almost too easy in all honesty, back then everyone believed anything that was in front of them and could not help but do what they were told through fear of the unknown."

Ellie turned back to Abijah, "If you hadn't started all this, if you had just left everything alone," she closed her eyes, tears forming now. "All people want, is to survive and be happy. In both worlds. Why can't we just carry on living as we always have?" Turning to face the Man, the one who was with her she asked, "Why do you want to destroy?"

There was a pause, broken only by the faint chanting from Abijah on the breeze.

"Because, Eleanor," the Man spoke after a short while, "I want Imaginari to have what your world has had for thousands of years – physical form. I want it to thrive in ways that we can only dream of and your world takes for granted. If that means ending your world then so be it. So be it." There was a determined tone to his voice now, he was clearly relishing the thought of destruction. "Your world is polluted and in decline, it will no doubt end soon anyway so why not do it in a way that gives another world a chance?"

Ellie could not believe this, "Are you really suggesting, that because we have made some mistakes, which I may add we are now trying to rectify, we deserve to be exterminated and have everything taken away?"

"Perhaps. I believe you had your chance, and now it is ours for the taking. You out number us, but we possess power that you cannot comprehend or understand, your world must end for ours to thrive."

Ellie stared at him. She knew he was driven and evil, but she had never heard him talk this way before, the time he had spent pondering and building this plan had clearly affected him.

"But now Eleanor, we must observe."

Ellie wiped her eyes as she turned, she needed to focus, drive her emotions out and stay calm. "I've beaten you before, and I will again," she muttered to herself under her breath, not caring if he heard her or not.

The scene had now changed slightly, the Man in the representation had floated over and was now in front of Abijah who was bowing down at his master's feet. The sight of someone acting in such a callous way was heart-breaking for Ellie, she moved closer to hear what was being said.

"So, you understand what you must do my loyal follower?" the Man asked of Abijah.

"Yes, my master," came the soft, trembling reply. "We must build a monument to your power, a way for you to protect us from the evils in your world."

"Good, good," came the commanding voice of the Man.

For a moment, Ellie forgot that this was not real, even she trembled at his tone.

"This monument must stand the test of time; it will require the care and protection of people from your world. You must choose these people carefully; you must trust them as I trust you," he continued.

"I will choose my most trusted companions from the village," Abijah said, his voice muffled as his face was almost touching the ground through bowing. "I have already begun speaking to them of my visions and belief in you, master. They will help me and do what you have asked."

"The first stones must be in place before the first full moon of winter, which is when my world will strike against yours. I will help you, but first you must get your people to get the stones in the positions on this map."

Ellie had not noticed the stone with the carvings on until this point in the conversation. She moved around the two men, still listening to Abijah tremble in fear of his new master. After she had manoeuvred around them, she was able to see a large stone carving on the floor beside Abijah. It was about the size of a dinner plate, and on it scratched into the stone was a symbol Ellie knew all too well. A Large 'M' inside of a circle. She turned her attention back to the two men, Abijah was standing now facing the Man eye to eye.

"Yes master, the stones are ready to be placed. They were carved out of this place as you requested, one at a time over a period of days. After each had been carved, we waited overnight and as you foresaw the stone reappeared meaning each of the five is now identical not just in source, but in shape, size, and weight. Down to the last crack, identical."

"Very good Abijah, very good," the Man taunted. "Once they are in place, dug in as far as you can, you must come back here to summon me once more. Then I shall join the stones together for you through the Earth creating a powerful connection, this will allow you to start protecting your world from the evil in mine."

Ellie looked back at the Man that had presented her with this, "So, they are the five-stone keys that are around the village I assume? They all came from here?"

"Yes, Eleanor. They were all carved from the same area, you heard Abijah say that they carved one and then waited as overnight the stone reappeared. This was me creating the stone each night, burning through energy from my world to do so, this was my sacrifice."

"Sacrifice?" Ellie interrupted, "Hardly, you were building something to help destroy our world, it's only because you got it slightly wrong that we survived isn't it?"

"Correct," he replied. "But I will not make the same mistake again, I will be victorious."

"You already said that," Ellie replied, her confidence returning by the second. "So, if this is the moment the keys were made, what else can we see?" She was trying to stall a little but was also curious that there may be a way to find out more about his plan and how to stop it. "Where else can we go?"

"This recreation is vast and if you enjoy it here so much, I think I can make it even more believable and life-like for you."

He floated towards Ellie. She took a step back expecting to feel the cold hill behind her but there was nothing, the world she had been observing was fading to purple smoke again, and she could now only make out the outlines of the hill, the stone, Abijah, and the Man. Standing out against the backdrop was the real Man though, he was gliding ever closer reaching out a hand, a finger. Closer, closer, Ellie stood firm and braced for whatever was about to happen.

"I'm going to enjoy this," he said calmly, "for you are now going to experience a small amount of my power."

He was nearly within touching distance now, his finger reaching out to Ellie's forehead. Her instinct was to run, scream, or defend herself but she fought against it to look at him, she wanted to defy him as much as she could. His finger reached her head, and after a moment of chill from the initial touch, there was nothing. Then a blinding searing pain spread from the point her head met his finger through her body. She screamed out and collapsed to her knees, even though this broke the contact the pain did not subside. Ellie curled up into a ball begging for the pain to stop, her ears were ringing, and her heart was pounding. Over the noise in her head she heard the voice of the Man, gloating and full of glee.

"This is not the end for you, Eleanor Fields. But you will need to fight hard to make it to the next painful chapter in your short existence."

Then, silence. The pain had stopped, the ringing subsided. She lay still for a few moments to make sure everything in her body was returning to normal. She pulled apart her arms and peered through the gap. Green grass, she could see and indeed feel it all around and under her. She unfolded her arms fully, opened her eyes and turned onto her back to look up at the sky. Clear blue with no purple smoke in sight. She lay still for a further moment, bracing for the Man to reappear and inflict more pain on her. Nothing happened. She decided to pull herself to her feet, after doing so she brushed off the grass that had stuck to her clothes and looked around. She was exactly where she was in the recreation moments earlier except this time, it felt real. Ellie turned frantically wanting to check that she was back where she wanted to be. There were no fences though, no warning signs and more noticeably no rock Statue Of Mow. This was real though, or at least it felt real. The wind on her face and the ground beneath her feet all felt real not like before when she had been in his recreation. In those situations, Ellie had the feeling of floating whenever she moved. This was very solid. Stepping backwards, Ellie tripped and fell landing on her back facing the sky.

"That certainly never happened before," she moaned out loud, winded from the fall. She lifted herself up onto her elbows and looked at what had tripped her. What she saw made her take a sharp intake of breath in shock. It was a circular stone, about the size of a dinner plate with the symbol of Mow scratched into it. Panicking, Ellie backed away on her elbows and this time was able to feel the cold Earth of the alcove behind her. She pulled her knees into her chest and tried to calm her breathing down. "It's not real, it can't be. He can't have sent me back in time, that's impossible," she said to herself over and over to try and focus her mind. She looked down, she was still wearing her own clothes, if she had been sent back in time this would cause a problem of its own as she did not exactly look the part. Trainers were not known for their primeval look and feel. Without moving, she looked up and around her again, she was sat in the carved-out hole in the hilltop that she had just been looking at. Listening hard she heard the sound of footsteps coming up the hill, she had to move fast to hide whilst she worked out what to do next, all she knew was that she could not be found dressed like this. She stood and looked around, there was a large tree to her left that would suffice for the immediate danger. The footsteps were closer now and Ellie was sure that the owner of them would appear above the crest of the hill any moment. She began to run towards the tree hoping against hope that she would reach it before being seen. Ellie glanced over her shoulder to check if she would make it and in that split second when she was not looking forwards, she lost her footing and fell. Tumbling to the floor banging her head and scraping arms and legs Ellie fell into a roll and then came to a stop in a heap just before the tree. Looking round, she could now see the owner of the footsteps that had instilled her with so much fear. They belonged to Abijah, and he was looking straight at her.

CHAPTER 4

Ellie stared back, unable to move or breathe. She felt compelled to stay perfectly still, as if doing so made her invisible, the way a spider acts when you see one move across the floor. Still he looked at her, his brown eyes clear in the sunlight, but he did not move.

Why aren't you moving or saying anything, Ellie thought to herself.

When Abijah still had not moved she started to untangle herself and eventually stood. Brushing herself down she kept her eyes on him, he did not move and had barely even blinked. Ellie took a step forward, fully aware that she was taking a risk. A teenage girl wearing trainers, a crop top, and shorts, walking around in whatever time period this was towards a man who was terrified to his very core of a mysterious ghostly figure that had come to him in a vision at night.

"Hello," she said softly, trying not to startle him. Nothing. "My name is Eleanor. My friends call me Ellie, I think I'm a bit lost can you help me?"

She figured that going for the sympathy route may be the best course of action at this stage. He did not move though; he was just looking at her. Ellie moved closer, taking one cautious step after another treading carefully over the firm ground. After a few moments, she was right in front of Abijah, no more than an arm's length away in front of him.

"Can you understand me?" she asked, tilting her head to one side as she did so.

Without warning he shouted at the top of his voice, "Hail the Man Of Mow," dropped to his knees and started bowing repeatedly.

Ellie jumped back in shock, looking down at him she replied, "No, I'm not the Man. Stand up, please stop and stand up."

He ignored her, Ellie took a few steps to the side and knelt beside him. Instinctively she reached out a hand to comfort him, hesitated for a moment and then lowered her hand to gently rest on his shoulder. It passed straight through, as if he was made of air. There was no resistance nor change in temperature. Ellie stared at her own hand, then tried the other to be sure but the same thing happened. Deciding to try something different, she stood and walked through Abijah. Nothing. She felt nothing, and he did not change his position. Immediately, whilst still a little confused, Ellie relaxed as it was clear that he could neither see, feel, nor hear her. She turned to look in the direction he was bowing, there floating a short distance away in the direction Ellie had been running to, was the Man himself. Ellie considered, then deciding to test her theory marched towards the floating figure she had grown to loath.

"Hey, Man Of Mow," she shouted. "Yeah, you, the one floating there like the ghost that you are, I want a word with you. Who do you think you are manipulating people's minds like this?"

By this point, she was standing in front of him and he had not moved or said a word. Ellie closed her eyes and took one final step to pass through the Man. Again, nothing. She bent and put her hands on her knees breathing deep breaths of relief. Whilst she still did not know exactly what was going on, and why she could hear and touch the world but not the people in it, the thought that she could not be seen or heard either was a comforting one. After a few moments, she stood and turned, the Man and Abijah were now deep in discussion over at the area Ellie had first arrived at. They were standing near the stone symbol of Mow. Ellie headed over to listen to them as they talked.

"Yes master. The five stones are in place just as you asked, ready for you," Abijah stated, quite calmly Ellie thought.

"Good, then tonight I shall join them and then you will be able to prepare for the final step. Is the child ready?"

Even though Ellie was pretty sure this was not real, and they could not hurt her, his voice and words put her on edge like she had never experienced before. Ellie moved closer; she was now standing almost between the two men like a parent between two squabbling children.

"Yes, Elizabeth is prepared and ready for when the time comes. At the first full moon of winter the child will be offered up to secure our future."

"It is required and will be remembered," the Man replied, then without warning he turned and floated away from Abijah.

"When will you return?" Abijah called after him.

The Man stopped, turned, and spoke in a loud but calm voice. "Tonight, I shall join your keys through the Earth. Then I shall watch over the child to ensure nothing happens to it. You shall not hear from me again unless your faith waivers. If we succeed, on the first full moon of winter you will witness the power I have told you about. Then, you must build Abijah. Build so that your world remains safe."

Then he faded and disappeared. Ellie was piecing all of this together now. Along with what she knew from her previous visits like this she now realised and understood how he had hoodwinked the villagers into supporting him.

"Best magic trick ever," Ellie said aloud, forgetting herself for a moment.

Abijah had started to move away too, twisting his hands in his palms as if nervous but otherwise acting normally. He was about to disappear over the edge of the hill when Ellie called after him.

"Hey, don't go," he kept walking. "Of course, you will keep walking," Ellie scolded herself, "You can't hear me."

She decided to follow him and moved in the direction that he had walked over the edge of the hill. To Ellie's surprise and amazement, she was able to keep going. As she moved forward the horizon seemed to move away as well. Looking around her she soon realised that it appeared she could walk anywhere. Initially she caught up with Abijah whose pace had quickened. Then to test out her surroundings she moved off to the side and walked in the same direction as him but through the trees on the right, she could still see him but was now a distance away.

"This is madness," she said to herself. Normally Ellie was very conscious of keeping her thoughts to herself but given that nobody could hear her she concluded that she may as well speak aloud. Deciding to push the limits, Ellie ran back towards Abijah and crossed his path immediately in front of him. If this had been real then he absolutely would have noticed, stopped, and maybe even fallen over from the potential impact. Nothing. Deciding that there was no way she could be heard or noticed, and feeling reasonably safe at the same time, Ellie decided to walk with Abijah to see where he was going. After a short while they began to approach a small hut. With no modern points of reference Ellie did not know where she was in the village and could not place herself on a mental map. Abijah walked confidently towards the hut, although Ellie could not really tell where the hut's land began and ended, she just followed along. He approached the doorway and lifted the rag of a curtain that covered it.

"Elizabeth?" he called out softly.

"Come in, but no loud noises, I just got her off," came the soft female reply.

He entered; Ellie followed although she was able to walk through the curtain rather than having to move it.

"How is she?" Abijah asked, "any better?"

He was standing in the middle of the room, to the left was an area surrounded by sheets and rags. Ellie assumed this is where a child was, to the right a woman was bent over a bucket of water apparently washing something.

"No Abijah, she is not," came the short reply. "You already knew that though, so why are you really here?" she stood and turned to face him.

To Ellie she looked exhausted, but also distraught as if the weight of the world was on her shoulders and there was nothing she or anyone else could do about it. Abijah took a step forward, but she raised her hand to stop him.

"What do you want Abijah?" Elizabeth demanded.

"I came to see how you are. I know there isn't anything I can do, and I know that you blame me, but I still care for you and want to look after you."

Ellie positioned herself between the two, she felt sorry for him. He was doing what he believed to be necessary it was just a tragedy that the child would be lost.

"At least, lost at this point in his story," Ellie said out loud. "She reappears but they don't know that yet." Ellie was recalling the story the Man had told her before, that the child had reappeared after vanishing from the hilltop.

In this moment of self-wonderment, Ellie had lost focus on the room and the atmosphere had certainly changed, they were shouting at each other now.

"You brought this down on us with your weird words and strange predictions, Abijah," Elizabeth screamed. "You sit on top of your hill and look down on us all as if we are to do your bidding and not question you. When will you sacrifice something? When will you have unbearable pain running through your body at every moment?" She was crying with a mixture of rage, fear, and loss at this point.

Abijah seemed at a loss for words. Ellie took a step back to survey the scene. The hut was not much bigger than the average modern living room. The area surrounded by sheets and rags that she could not see into was to the left, there was what looked like a bed and then a store area filled with small boxes and trinkets to the right. The woman, Elizabeth, had been in that area with the bucket of water washing what appeared to be a shirt. This was in the hand that she was using to gesture the most to Abijah and as such was spraying water everywhere. He was not saying much, Ellie could understand why. He believed he was the messenger, but if the Man had not presented himself to anyone else in the village then why should they believe it was not him just trying to assume control over them? This was a primitive time and Ellie knew that back then what was feared most was the unknown and anything unexplained. The Man had told her that before. She moved to the side, leaving them to argue as it appeared to be going nowhere. Crossing over to the sheets she stepped through them, it was taking some getting used to this moving through things. After a brief wash of white,

CHAPTER 4

Ellie could see a bundle of cloths and rags around a sleeping baby. She could not be sure, but it certainly looked like the one she had seen in a previous vision up on the hill.

"Joanna," she said aloud. "You have no idea what is going on do you? Probably for the best. Ignore the yelling and be brave. It will scare you, but I promise you will be back here before you know it with everyone loving you." Ellie kneeled to get closer. "I know you can't hear me, but this is so weird seeing and talking to my great, great, great, great ancestor like this. I wonder what you grow up to be like, would I recognise you?" Ellie pondered this, this was not real, and she had not travelled in time. If she had, would she recognise anything? Or would it all be normal and a blur? She stood, said goodbye to Joanna and left through the curtain. They had gone. Ellie moved quickly towards the door and to her relief she could see Abijah moving along the path, Elizabeth just glaring at him with her arms crossed. Ellie went and stood by Elizabeth for a moment and looked at her. There were tears streaming down her face now, her eyes were red and puffy. Ellie could not be sure, but it looked as if she was trembling with what she assumed was rage.

"What has gone on between you to cause this?" she asked, "Is it just because of your daughter? Where is her father?" Then it hit her. "Abijah is her father! Of course, that is why the Man picked him and then her to test him," Ellie continued. "You can't see the Man, so you blame him for casting out your daughter, I wonder what he has given you for his reasons, the truth? Made up something? Only you and he know I guess." Ellie felt a sinking feeling in her heart. This was all the Man's fault, not Abijah's. She felt sorry for him, he would feel so trapped and lost. She turned and looked in the direction Abijah had moved off in. "Poor family."

There was a sound of a baby crying from inside the hut and Elizabeth went back inside. The sun was moving slowly down now, Ellie guessed it was mid-afternoon.

"I want to be back on the hill tonight, to see the Man," she said. "Seen as I am here and have no way to get out, I may as well look around."

With a final look at Elizabeth's hut, Ellie turned and moved along the path to investigate the village as it was before all the madness ensued.

There were a couple of huts but before long Ellie had made it all the way down the hill with very little to see. Cattle and sheep here and there, a few people but nothing that really caught her eye. Ellie paused, turning to look back up the hill as she did so. Untouched by modern houses it was a sight to behold. Whilst she still had no modern points of reference, she was sure that she would have passed where the railway and canal would eventually be by this point. It was just a perfect untouched hill of green, standing proud over the landscape in the same way it does today.

"Right, Eleanor," she told herself. "What next? You are apparently stuck in a very large real looking recreation of the hill you now call home. You don't know how to get out so what do you know?" she sat and thought. She quickly realised she did not know a lot, other than an assumption that Abijah and Elizabeth were a couple, Joanna was their daughter, and tonight the Man was going to do something with the keys. "The keys," she exclaimed. "Go find one of those, then get back to the hilltop before nightfall. That's a plan."

Feeling confident and for some reason reassured by this, Ellie set off across the field to try and find one of the five keys in the village. This initially proved to be a challenge, she knew that the stones were in a circle around the village but had no idea how far up or down the hill they were. Thinking tactically, Ellie focused hard to think how the hill looked from her house. Obviously, there was no folly to focus on, but the hill was still there none the less. Once she had got the hill at what she believed to be the right height she walked in a circle keeping it the same distance to her right. The logic being that eventually she should reach one of the stones. It appeared that luck was on her side, for a short while later Ellie came across a small hut with what appeared to be a stone that looked the same as the one in her garden just outside it. As she got closer she quickened her pace, the sun was getting lower in the sky now and she still wanted to make it up the hill before nightfall. It was odd walking here though, there seemed to be no difference between walking up or down hill in terms of effort required. This meant that whilst she was aware she had been walking for a while she did not feel worn out. Ellie approached the stone, now she was close enough to see all of the markings and edges she was certain it was one of the five stone keys. She reached out to touch it, but her hand went straight through the stone.

"Of course, you can't touch it, Eleanor," she scolded herself.

Resting on her knees, she focused hard on the stone, it had to be one of the stones.

"I see the stone is ready for tonight," a rough male voice came from behind her.

Startled, Ellie stood and whirled around. She found herself facing a man, quite a bit taller than she was and well built. He looked strong, mean, and not very happy.

Ellie composed herself and faced the man, but before she could say anything a female voice spoke from behind her.

"Well, you know Abijah, once he sets his mind to something, it tends to happen. Why the four of us though I have no idea."

Ellie turned. A woman had appeared in the doorway of the hut. Compared to Abijah and Elizabeth, these two looked positively modern and would not have looked out of place in her own time. Less the rags for clothes of course.

"That's true Isabella, that's true," the man replied. "There must be a reason though, why else would he offer up their own daughter to save us all?"

This confirmed Ellie's thoughts, Abijah was Joanna's father which also meant he was her ancestor too. Ellie did not know how to process this thought though, the idea of a parent giving up a child was difficult for her to process but given what she knew about the Man and how he worked, she understood why he was so scared of him.

The woman, who Ellie now knew as Isabella, pursed her lips, "So, you believe him do you, Thomas? You believe that he has had contact with a god who has demanded that he give up his own daughter?"

Ellie was piecing it all together now, these were two more council members. As soon as she made the connection, she was able to place their faces from the top of the hill. It also confirmed her thoughts that this was a stone key for the folly.

Thomas shifted slightly, clearly uneasy with this line of questioning. "I think there is no love stronger than that of family, so whatever is making him do this must be terrifying."

Isabella was apparently disarmed by this comment, "Yes, that is true. But do we know that he is telling us the truth? Or is it because he wanted a son and is rejecting a daughter? Have you considered that, Thomas?" Isabella seemed determined again now, any temporary relief for Thomas had been lifted.

"Can you really think any parent would do that? It's not like he has been acting normal of late is it?" Thomas replied.

"Well, tonight will tell us won't it? When these so-called keys actually do something."

She gestured towards the stone that Ellie was standing by, Ellie looked at it and could completely understand why everyone was so confused and angry now. It was insane.

"Yes, we will," Thomas replied. "Are we going with him, or are we watching from afar?"

For a moment Isabella said nothing. Then retorted, "I will go where Elizabeth goes, she has my support tonight."

With that, she turned and entered the hut.

Thomas sighed and turned to leave, only pausing to call over his shoulder, "Nice seeing you Isabella, see you soon."

Then he walked away.

"What a strange group of villagers they are," Ellie mused to herself out loud. "Still, different time I guess."

She looked up at the sun which had now started to turn a faint shade of orange as it dipped below the horizon. Then, defiantly and with a certain level of confidence, she too headed away and up the hill to see what would happen tonight.

Given that Ellie could not be seen or heard, she decided that she wanted the best seat in the house for whatever the Man was up to this evening. So she climbed to the very top of the hill, the place where the folly stood today and that she herself had lay years before to defend the world. She sat cross legged on the very spot she had placed herself and looked down the ridge to where Abijah had been sitting. She had a good view, could see for miles but also had a perfect view of everything that would happen tonight. Ellie was also keen to see which of the other council members would arrive to support Abijah, or indeed to see what would happen if they challenged him. To her surprise, not long after nightfall they all appeared over the hill together. They approached Abijah and Ellie focused hard to try and hear what was said between them.

"Thank you all for coming," Abijah said first. He looked at Elizabeth, "I know this has been hard for you, for all of us. But it is for the best."

"So you keep saying," Isabella interrupted. "Get on with it."

He turned to face her, "I cannot speed up the will of the Man, he does as he pleases. I am but his voice in our world and we must do as he commands."

"As he commands?" Thomas asked. "Why Abijah? Why are you following him and listening to him?" There was a tone of desperation to his voice.

"He has foretold of someone from his world, the spirit world Imaginari, that wishes to destroy ours. He has told me that if we do not act and we allow this evil in, we and our world will perish to smoke and ash."

"His world, Imaginari?" Elizabeth queried. "Why can't they deal with this, why our world? Why us? Why here?"

All valid questions Ellie felt, even with her extended knowledge of events to come she did not know the answers.

"This hill we live upon is special. It stands alone and not only alone but at the exact point in his world where there is a weakness," Abijah explained. "It seems that energy flows from our world to theirs and has for centuries but when this evil tried to penetrate, all it could do was weaken the barrier. This spot is where that weakness began and still exists."

"So, what do we have to do? What is the idea here Abijah?" This was the only person not to have spoken, a small, stout, fair-haired woman.

"Philippa," Abijah replied. "What he needs from us is simple. We have already placed the five key stones around the village. Tonight, he will join them through the Earth to ensure their strength for eternity. Then, on the first full moon of winter, he will take our daughter and use her pure energy to seal the weakness between worlds. The five stones will hold this firm, but, if this works, we will then need to build a lock to enforce the keys and keep this evil at bay forever." Silence fell over the group, then Abijah concluded, "This is what the Man has foretold, and all I can do is deliver his messages. So now, we wait."

He turned and sat once more, cross legged facing up at the peak where Ellie was sat. It looked as though he was waiting for her to do something, as if she was putting on a show. To Ellie's surprise, the other members of the council sat behind him, so they could all see. From where she was, they looked like children in school waiting for an assembly or for a teacher to start singing the morning hymns.

Ellie had no idea how much time passed, but it was not short. The group below her moved and chatted quietly. All except Abijah who stared, quiet and focused, indeed Ellie herself was starting to get a little bored waiting for something to happen. She was passing the time by examining her palm, it still had the faint markings left by the rock that had trapped her what seemed like a very long time ago.

"What is that?" she asked out loud, running her fingers from the other hand over it. It did not hurt, could hardly notice to the touch, but she knew it was there and something had changed. As if a pencil sketch had transferred to her palm somehow. Ellie lowered her palm and looked out at the group. They were still there looking expectantly at the sky above where she sat.

Then, out of nowhere and without warning, it happened. There was a thunderous bolt of light from the cloudless sky that came crashing down just up the rise from where Ellie was sat. It made her jump, even though she knew she was safe. She leapt to her feet and turned to face the direction of the impact. There, floating in glorious glowing white was the Man Of Mow.

"My loyal followers," his deep voice boomed, the loudest Ellie had ever heard it. "You have come here tonight to witness the beginning of the protection of your world. If you stay loyal to me, and you do as I ask, all will be safe for eternity."

Ellie turned to face the group, they were all bowing, praying even, to the apparent deity that had appeared before them.

The Man spread his arms and continued, "I am here before you to build on your precious work. Abijah informs me that the five keys are in place and are ready for me. Tonight, I shall join them through the Earth to make a strong bond. Then, at the first full moon of winter we shall banish this evil and seal the portal with the building of a lock."

Ellie scoffed, she knew that this was him playing to the crowed to get what he wanted, and it was an impressive way to do it. She herself was in awe of him, this was the first time she had seen him look so powerful and daunting. Turning to face the man, she braced herself for what was to happen next.

He rose into the air like a glowing balloon, the bright light that shone down from him lit up the top of the hill in its entirety. So much so that the group of villagers and Ellie had to shield their eyes. Once he had reached a height that Ellie felt was about the height that the folly would become, he spread his arms. The moment he did so a bolt of light shot down from the sky, going through the Man and into the ground not too far from where Ellie was standing. The moment it hit the ground the Earth shook, rattling Ellie to her core as she watched. Glancing down the hill, she could see the fear etched on the faces of the five people below, the Man was working his story into their minds and using fear to bend them to his will. Looking up at him, she could see that he was slowly turning, as he did so the beam of light into the ground was pulsating. Then, with a final rumble from the ground Ellie noticed another beam of light reaching up from the horizon. She focused her eyes and looked closely, it was reaching out from the ground and heading towards the Man floating in the sky. Looking round, she saw there were four more, all of them reaching up to him forming a star shape.

"The five keys," she said to herself. "That's the energy from the keys, he is joining them up exactly where the folly will be built. So, the energy going into the ground must be pushing through the Earth to get to them. He is using the whole hill."

As she and the villagers watched, the five beams of light now pulsated in time with the energy flowing into the ground and were almost at the Man, who was still slowly turning as he floated above the ground. At the moment they made contact with him the light was so blinding Ellie had to look away. It was as if a spotlight had been turned on right in front of her eyes. When it had subsided and she was able to look once more, the sight was terrifyingly beautiful. The Man had moved away now, his work apparently completed, and he was floating down towards the group of villagers. Where he was floating before, there was now an arc of light and energy. Seemingly flowing down from the sky and into the ground, through the Earth and out at the five stones. Then moving back through the air to meet the beam from the sky, the same sort of shape made by a circus tent being held up by a single pole. It was flowing steadily now, the pulsating had calmed and looked as if it was stable. Ellie felt that if she did not know what it actually was, and what it meant for the future, she would have found it to be very beautiful indeed. She turned her attention to the group of villagers below that were bowing once more with the Man floating not far in front of them.

"It is done," the Man said softly. "The energy flow is stable, and the five keys are supporting the protection. This should be enough for now to start the process of protecting your world, from Imaginari."

"Thank you, great Man," Abijah replied. He seemed pleased that something had happened and that it appeared to be positive as well. "Now we wait?" he asked.

"Yes, now you wait," came the reply. "If all is well, this will be enough and after the first full moon in winter you will be able to start work on the lock, the structure to reinforce this energy."

He gestured around him. The beams of light were fading now, dimming as though weakening.

"Where have they gone?" Elizabeth asked, "Has it stopped?"

The Man moved in front of her. "Naïve woman," he shouted sternly. "The energy has not stopped it is simply returning to its raw form. The energy always exists and always flows, it is still there but is no longer visible." He stopped, and silence fell over the group, "Do not question me again."

With that he turned and floated up and away from them, above where Ellie was standing and down the other side of the hill.

"You will not see me again if our plan works," he called back. "But if your faith stalls or your belief fades, I shall know, and you shall face the full power of my wrath."

With one last look at the now fear filled first council, Ellie turned and followed the Man. She did not know why, but it felt like the right thing to do. She quickly caught up with him and walked directly behind him along a path that had been worn into the grass. To Ellie's surprise, he was talking to himself.

"Fools. I have them exactly where I want them, they do not understand what they have done for they have doomed their world. On the first full moon I will use the pure child's energy to rip open the portal and absorb all the energy from this miserable world into my own. They will not get a chance to build that stupid lock, Abijah believes he is their saviour when really he has -" then he abruptly stopped. So did Ellie although she was startled at the sudden stop that he had made. Without warning he turned to face exactly where Ellie stood. She turned and looked behind her but there was nothing and nobody there. She faced him once more and he was still staring right through her. They stayed like this for a moment or two, Ellie was confused as she knew that he could not see her, so what was he looking at? She moved away and headed in the direction he was looking at, towards the trees. There really was nothing there. Then, without warning he spoke once more.

"I see you; I do not know you, but I see you. I know I cannot deal with you now, but no matter, even if you are here you cannot stop me."

He turned and carried on in the direction he was going.

Confused, Ellie hurried after him. He was moving silently

now as if concerned he was being listened to. Before long Ellie realised they were walking in the same direction and along the same route that she had been earlier today. They were walking towards the Statue Of Mow area of the hill, where Abijah's house was, and where her day had begun. True enough they were soon back at the small area that Abijah had claimed and where the single rock stood. Although it was no longer a single rock. It had now transformed into the collection of rocks that Ellie knew and recognised from her time in the village. This matched perfectly the one that she had touched.

"A masterpiece," the Man said. "It formed perfectly and gives me a nice way to move between worlds without anyone knowing. That fool Abijah will help me by carrying on setting up home here," he chuckled. "Now, time to return."

The Man moved towards the rocks. When he reached them, he appeared to travel through them into the rock face.

"Now what?" Ellie asked to nobody. She moved towards the rock in hope of following but instead was butted away by a solid rock face. She took a step back and looked at the rock. She then approached it and felt the surface, nothing. No buzz or hum was emitting from it this time and she was at a loss as to what to do next. As she pulled her hand away, she felt a small spark, just a little one but enough to notice. Jumping back, she looked at her palm and the mark that was there previously. It was still there but now had a purple shimmer over it, as if it was glowing in the moonlight. Ellie looked from her palm, to the rock, and back again. She could not be sure but the rock appeared to have a faint glimmer of purple to it as well.

"Surely not?" she exclaimed and knelt closer to the surface of the rock.

Reaching out she compared the mark on her palm to that of the grain on the surface of the rock sliding around to try and find a match. It took a few moments but eventually she found a place where the grain looked similar. Taking a deep breath, she lined her palm up and pushed hard on the rock. There was searing pain and blinding light. Ellie screamed and then found herself hurtling backwards and landing on something soft. She opened her eyes and looked up at the sky, it was blue and clear.

"Excuse me," a female voice said. "Could you get off me please?"

Startled, Ellie realised the something soft was a person and immediately got up. She looked around. Everything looked familiar once again, the warning signs were back, and everything looked as it was when she had been walking earlier that day. Judging by the sun and the heat, she had not been away for that long in terms of time either.

"Sorry," Ellie said. "I, er, didn't see you."

"No, clearly you didn't," the girl said.

Ellie turned to look at her and immediately felt the bottom fall out of her stomach in shock. "Who, who are you? What are you doing here?" she asked, her voice quiet and shaking with fear.

Ellie felt weak at the knees and was struggling to breathe now too.

The girl who had now paused dusting herself down looked up at Ellie. She had blonde hair and blue eyes, wearing a crop top and shorts. Tilting her head to one side she replied, "I was walking, killing time before meeting my girlfriend Annabelle later. It was a pleasant walk until interrupted by you." She stopped and patted herself down once more, "and in answer to your other question, my name is Emilia Fields. Now who are you?"

CHAPTER 5

Emilia.

In almost every way Emilia Fields was a typical seventeen-year-old girl. Just over two years ago her family had moved out of London to the picturesque village of Mow Cop to support her mother, Katherine, who had got a new job in the area. She was close to her father, Nicholas, and the three of them had set up home and settled in over the last two years. The Fields family home was on a small road in the village, it had three floors and Emilia had the bedroom that was in the loft space, meaning she had her own bathroom and space to do what she wanted with. She had settled into school and made a close group of friends. In that time, she had also forged a relationship with Annabelle, a dark-haired girl in her year at school and they had been together for a little over two years. Life was good for Emilia, her friends, and family. The only thing that made Emilia different to other teenage girls was what had happened shortly after moving to the village. After being drawn into a cult like council, Emilia had faced off against a spirit known in the village as the Man. With the help of her friends, she had bested him and saved the village and the world. Since then, life had progressed normally although Emilia did not appreciate the level of appreciation she got for what she had done. She found it irritating and annoying that people would not leave her alone about it. Indeed, there were times when she gently wished that she had failed, or something had gone wrong with their plan just to stop the flow of gratitude coming her way. All she wanted was to carry on with her life and enjoy herself.

It was a sunny summer Saturday and Emilia had just finished work at the local supermarket. As she left Annabelle was waiting for her holding an ice cream each for them both. She walked over, gave Annabelle a kiss and a quick cuddle and took the ice cream that was hers.

"Thanks, I need this today," Emilia said.

"Welcomes lovely," Annabelle replied. "Bad day?"

Emilia sighed, "You have no idea. All I want to do is go home and rest," she put her head on Annabelle's shoulder.

"Well, you can do that for a little while," Annabelle replied. "But you need to have your game face on for the barbecue tonight."

Emilia sighed, "Yeah I know, lots of people to chat to. Some that I like, some that I don't. The joys. Come on let's go and get this over with."

The two girls headed for the bus and then back to Emilia's house, it was only a short journey and before long they were off the bus again and walking down the street towards Emilia's home. She stopped and turned to face the folly on the hill. At first Annabelle did not notice and carried on walking, when she did notice though she turned and called back to Emilia.

"What's up, you forgotten how to walk or something?"

Emilia glared at Annabelle, "No, Annabelle I have not," she replied harshly. "I am simply contemplating how different the world would be if I had done what I actually wanted to do and let the Man win. How much simpler things would have been if I had just rolled over and let him win, smashed the stones, done nothing. Anything other than what I actually did would be marvellous thank you."

Annabelle's mouth dropped open in shock, "Babe, I was just teasing."

"Well, don't. I've had enough of it."

With that, Emilia stormed off towards home. Annabelle, pausing to try and process exactly what had just happened then quickly followed. The two girls entered the house in silence, then Emilia slammed the front door shut and stormed upstairs leaving Annabelle looking upset and confused in the doorway.

"What's all the slamming about?" came Katherine's voice from the kitchen. She then appeared in the doorway, "You ok Annabelle?" she asked kindly.

Annabelle looked at her, tears forming in her eyes. "I, I was only teasing her about walking and she, she just stormed away saying something about how she wished nothing had ever happened," she covered her face and burst into tears.

Katherine, who was very fond of Annabelle, hurried over and wrapped her in a cuddle to comfort her.

"Hey, come on, come and have a cup of tea and tell me what happened. I'll talk to Emilia when she has calmed down ok?"

Katherine led Annabelle into the kitchen and put the kettle on. As she did so Annabelle told her what had happened. Everything from the bad day at work to the comment after getting off the bus, focussing in particular on the part where she had wished that nothing had happened and that she had let the Man win. Katherine listened in silence waiting for her to finish.

"And then we came in and she stormed upstairs, and I don't know why or what I've done." Annabelle burst into tears again, "It's just I care about her so much and I feel that she is saying that she would rather we weren't together because if what happened hadn't happened then she wouldn't be with me," she sobbed.

"Well, we both know that's not true; she adores you Annabelle and you have helped her so much and we see how happy you both are together," Katherine comforted. "This is difficult for me to be in the middle of but let me go and talk to her and see what she says."

"You don't have to; I can just go and leave her here for your party. My mum and dad will be here soon, and I don't want them to see me like this."

"You'll do no such thing. Besides, it will be worse if they are here and you're not don't you think?" Katherine replied with a raised eyebrow and a smirk.

"I guess."

"Right, stay here, drink your tea and I will be back down shortly, with or without my daughter."

With that, Katherine left, Annabelle sipped her tea, wiping her eyes and trying to calm herself down. A short while later she had drunk her tea, and whilst still feeling sad and confused, she was starting to lift her spirits a little. She heard footsteps coming down the stairs and took a deep breath to steady herself for what may happen next. She heard the footsteps get closer and then a soft voice spoke.

"You going to let me see that pretty face?" Emilia asked, kindly.

Annabelle turned and faced her, doing her best to put on a brave face to hide her pink cheeks and puffy eyes. "Hi," she said, softly and cautiously.

"I didn't mean to upset you, Annabelle," said Emilia, "you're the best thing that has ever happened to me and I do not want to ruin that. I was just, I just feel," she stopped and scrunched her hands in a nervous fidget. "I just don't like the ongoing pressure from everybody else. And I guess it got on top of me. I'm sorry." She lowered her head in what appeared to be shame, "I didn't mean half of what I said, I promise. I just want a normal life."

"And you can have that," Annabelle interrupted. "We can have that, together, it's all over now. You did what you needed to do and if you never want to talk of it again then don't." She reached out a hand and took one of Emilia's, "You're special to me and I am here to protect you. We are on the same team," she squeezed Emilia's hand.

Emilia looked up and their eyes met. For a moment, they just simply looked at each other. Emilia was reminded how beautiful Annabelle is and Annabelle was reminded of Emilia's deep blue eyes. Emilia cracked first and smiled, instantly the tension between the two was released and they embraced in a hug that meant more to them both than they would ever admit to.

"I'll calm down, promise," Emilia said through tears.

"Just remember I'm with you, that's all I want," Annabelle replied.

"You two ok now?" Katherine asked as she appeared in the

doorway.

The girls pulled apart and nodded, each wiping their own faces to get the tears away.

"Good, now go and get ready then you can come and help us get the house ready. We will do the food, but we need you to do the drinks bin for outside ok?" Katherine was sympathetic but also a strong mother and she knew how to give out motherly orders.

The girls stood, and with Emilia leading Annabelle by the hand they left the kitchen to go and get ready.

Later that evening the party was in full swing, Emilia was socialising with the guests circulating as best she could. She was happy to chat to most, there were people from her parents work, the council that had helped her with the Man, and some friends from school too. Not to mention Annabelle's parents Jack and Audrey as well. Simon, one of Emilia's closest friends, was also there and was talking to Annabelle and Emilia.

"All I'm saying is I miss Sophie. Why is that so difficult to understand?" he asked.

"Yes Simon, we know," Emilia replied. "It's terrible that you can't see your girlfriend as often as you would like. What exactly would you like us to do about it?"

Annabelle and Simon looked at her astonished by her tone and language.

"Sorry, I didn't mean that," she immediately retracted. "I just meant that Annabelle and I see each other all the time, and that's great. But sometimes we get on each other's nerves don't we darling?"

She looked at Annabelle.

Initially Annabelle did not respond, but then clearly decided to agree, "Yes dear, we do," she walked away.

"What's her problem?" Simon asked.

"It's not her, it's me. I've been evil lately. I need to make it up to her! Any ideas?"

"Why not surprise her this week? Take her out for ice cream or something?" Simon suggested, "That's what I'd do anyway."

"That's a great idea," Emilia agreed. "I'll go and surprise her."
Emilia grinned and immediately felt better. She knew that Annabelle would support her, but she needed to buck her ideas up to keep everything happy and flowing.
"Other than missing each other, are you and Sophie ok?" she asked, wanting to change the subject.
"Yeah, we are, it's just difficult. I mean, we can't do the spontaneous thing can we? I can't surprise her with ice cream without planning a train journey and a stopover." There was a small hint of desperation in his voice at this and Emilia knew he was right.
"Suppose not, but you also know you have something you can depend on and that counts for a lot in a relationship."
It was not much, but it was all she could come up with at the time. She did feel sorry for Simon, this was the first real relationship he had ever had, and it was hard for them to be far apart.
"True," he replied. "And if it wasn't for you, I would never have met her," he pulled Emilia into a hug.
"Don't you start with the thanking me thing," she replied pulling away. "I'm happy you're happy, but I can't be dealing with any more thanks for stuff I didn't really do."
With that, Emilia stormed away leaving Simon shocked and unsure of what to say next. Emilia kept herself to herself for the remainder of the party. She spoke when she needed to and was always polite and pleasant, but otherwise she kept interactions to a minimum. Even when it came to going to bed, she kept the conversation with Annabelle short too. Annabelle's parents were going away for a couple of weeks for work, and they had arranged for Annabelle to stay with Emilia for the duration. Emilia had been very happy with this, but after the way she had acted she was just hoping she could get through it unscathed. Before long, the two girls were ready for bed, Emilia in hers and Annabelle on the blow-up bed.
"I'm sorry Annabelle," Emilia said softly from the comfort of her duvet. "I will figure out what is upsetting me, and I will fix it. Just know that it is not you, or us, and I will fight for you. Always."

"I know. I'm on your team too remember," Annabelle replied. "Now go to sleep and let's start putting all this behind us, deal?"

"Deal."

The two girls drifted off to sleep.

Emilia kept her word and for the next couple of days everything went back to normal, she even managed to stay calm when people tried to thank her or talk to her too much about how much she had done for them. The sun helped, she felt better when she could be outside relaxing. Today though, so far at least, she was indoors. She had done all the jobs she needed to do and was watching the world go by out of her round window in her room. Today was the day she was going to surprise Annabelle. She was going to go and wait for her outside work, but she still had a lot of time to kill. Eventually, Emilia decided to go and enjoy the sunshine. Shortly after making this decision she was in shorts and a crop top and ready to go. Given it was so hot she also filled a bottle of water. She decided to walk to the folly, to see if it could give her any inspiration to get her mindset changed about the world she now lived in. Retracing her steps, she followed the same route up the hill that she had the very first time she had walked up it not long after she had moved to Mow Cop. Before long she found herself sat on the very rock that Simon had disturbed her sunbathing. Emilia grinned to herself, he was silly but charming in his own way. For the first time in a while, Emilia felt a warm feeling inside about her life in the village. Deciding to go with it, she moved to face the folly and recalled how Simon had told her about it being on the north south divide.

"Where did he take me next?" she asked out loud. "The Man Of Mow. The rock one, the nice one," she concluded and decided to go and look at him once more.

Emilia walked past the folly and down off the peak of the hill. She walked along the hilltop path between farms and round the back of the hill to find the Man. There he was, or rather, there was the rock face that people called the Man Of Mow. She recalled Simon having to hold her head a certain angle to see him, now though she could see him for herself. It was just a pile of rocks but knowing what she now knew put them in a whole new light. These were just rocks though. Emilia looked at them, surrounded by warning signs and fences, the modern touches that often surround cliff faces and the like. Something felt odd though. As if she was being watched. She looked around, all around. Nobody and nothing.

"Anyone there?" she called out. Nothing.

She turned back to look at the rocks, she was sure she could hear a low hum.

"Rock's don't hum," she said to herself out loud.

Without thinking, she climbed over the barrier and moved towards the rock face, they were definitely humming. Buzzing even. Emilia took a drink of water, looked round once more to confirm there was nobody near her and then took a few cautious steps forward. As she got closer and without thinking, she reached out her hand. Palm outstretched towards the rock of the Man, she moved closer and closer. The buzzing was very real now, as if the rocks were generating an electric current. Her hand got closer and closer to the surface, and as it did so she felt an invisible barrier between her hand and the rock. She pushed forwards, it let her hand through as though pressing on a balloon. Then, just at the moment before her hand touched the surface of the rock the force changed and pulled her forwards. Emilia was pulled by her arm towards the rock, at the moment her palm touched the surface she was thrown backwards. There was a loud bang and before she knew what was happening, she was lying on the floor with something, or rather someone, lying on top of her.

"Excuse me," Emilia said. "Could you get off me please?" she asked in a stern voice.

Immediately the person, the girl that was on top of her, got off.

"Sorry," she said. "I, er, didn't see you."

"No, clearly you didn't," Emilia replied.

Emilia looked her up and down, and immediately realised that this girl was doing the same to her. Before she could say anything though, the other girl spoke first.

"Who are you? What are you doing here?" the girl asked.

Emilia was a little put out at this, you have just landed on me, and you ask me who I am, she thought to herself as she dusted herself down. Then she decided to be calm and polite. It was odd though, this girl had blonde hair, blue eyes, and was wearing a crop top and shorts. All of which were very similar to Emilia's. Tilting her head to one side Emilia replied, "I was walking, killing time before meeting my girlfriend Annabelle later. It was a pleasant walk until interrupted by you," she paused, patted herself down a little and decided to go on the offensive. "And in answer to your other question, my name is Emilia Fields. Now who are you?"

CHAPTER 6

Emilia.

Emilia stared at her, waiting for a response.

"Well?" she demanded. "Who are you?"

There was a pause then the girl finally replied, "Eleanor," then she paused again.

"Eleanor what?" Emilia demanded, her patience with this girl was wearing thin.

"Eleanor Smith," came the timid reply. "I live just around the corner, but I don't think we have met before?"

"No, we haven't. I would remember," Emilia replied confidently. "I would have remembered someone as infuriating as you," Emilia folded her arms in defiance.

"No need for that," Ellie replied. "It was an accident, it's not like I aimed for you or something is it?" She stormed past Emilia and headed to cross over the fence. Then she stopped and turned to face Emilia once more, "Did you say your girlfriends name was Annabelle?"

Emilia looked at her, "Yes, my girlfriends name is Annabelle, what of it?"

"Annabelle what?" Ellie enquired.

Emilia's eyes narrowed, she did not like the way this was going. "Annabelle Jones. Why? How do you know her?" She unfolded her arms and took a few steps towards Ellie.

"I, I thought I knew her is all," Ellie took a step backwards, clearly threatened by Emilia. "But I was wrong, I know Annabelle Granger, I thought it was the same girl is all. Small village, unusual name like Annabelle etc," Ellie smiled, it was a soft, weak smile but a smile none the less.

"Why do I have a feeling you are lying to me, Eleanor Smith?" Emilia asked, moving closer still to Ellie.

Ellie was backed against the fence now, she had nowhere to go. "I'm not. I was just mistaken is all," she pleaded.

Emilia was close now; the girls were almost touching noses. "If I find out you are lying to me," Emilia snarled. "I will find you, and you will regret ever bumping into me by that forsaken rock. Understand?"

Ellie nodded.

"Good," Emilia concluded, stepping back. "Now get lost."

With tears forming in her eyes, Ellie turned, climbed over the fence and hurried along the path.

Emilia glared after her, "Who are you really?" she asked out loud to nobody.

After a few minutes, Emilia decided to leave to go and meet Annabelle as she had planned. She headed away from the Statue Of Mow and down the path to the road, she needed to get to the bus stop to get into town to surprise Annabelle. Even though it was a glorious day and she had set off with such high hopes of her surprise and spending the late afternoon with Annabelle, the events that had unfolded were bothering her. The same few questions kept pinging round in her head.

Who was that girl? How did she know Annabelle? Where had she come from? Why were the rocks humming? Was this the Man, or something else?

No matter what she tried she could not change her train of thought and unfortunately for Emilia it was making her more and more jealous as she went along. The bus arrived and unsurprisingly it was empty, it was a warm weekday afternoon after all. She moved to the back of the bus and took a back-row seat by the window. As the bus pulled away, she looked out at the folly on the hill. She hated that thing, but could the girl be connected to the Man? Emilia stared at the folly until it was blocked from view by trees. Even after it had gone, she could not help but think that the events of today were connected somehow. It did not match any pattern of previous events though, she wracked her brain trying to find some distant memory that she may have missed or forgotten that would link the Man to the pile of rocks. The only reason they were called the Man Of Mow was because previous inhabitants of the village had named them so. She had never heard the Man speak of the rocks. When he had come to her in dreams and visions he had always focused on the folly, the lock, and the keys. Then there was the connection to Annabelle. If that girl was not connected to the Man or indeed to her, then how did she know of Annabelle?

"I don't for one second believe that you were looking for Annabelle Granger, Eleanor Smith," Emilia snarled to herself and the empty bus. "You're hiding something, and I am going to find out what it is. Starting with Annabelle."

Saying Annabelle's name out loud did soften her mood a little, she cared for Annabelle and knew that Annabelle cared for her in return, so she should not fear anything yet. But there was no denying that there was real anger inside her at the moment. Emilia spent the rest of the journey to town in silence, pondering and thinking of the best way to talk to Annabelle about what had happened. She needed to be careful, she could not start an argument or push Annabelle away. Emilia meant it when she had said that meeting her was the best thing to have happened to her, she could not risk changing or damaging that.

Emilia arrived at the bus stop in town a little earlier than she had originally planned, Annabelle did not finish for another two hours so she had some time to kill. Shopping, something that Emilia would normally love to do would have to suffice. She concluded that it may act as a distraction from her current mindset and help her relax. So as not to be noticed, she decided to stay at the opposite end of the shopping centre to where Annabelle worked. Before long Emilia was in full swing and moving through clothing shop aisles with ease. She had picked up a new top and some jeans before she knew it and was now contemplating getting a drink. After very little deliberation she decided to get an ice coffee. Taking stock of her finds she sat down in the coffeeshop window, even though it was inside a shopping centre it was still better to sit and watch the people go by than sit by a plain wall. She drank her drink and contemplated where to go next. As she was taking the last few sips, her eye was drawn to an odd shop across the centre walkway. It was one of those trinket shops that sells a little bit of everything but also nothing in particular. She stared at the shop, there appeared to be nobody in there other than the shopkeeper themselves. Emilia took a last gulp of drink, stood, and left the coffee shop to cross the walkway to the shop that had caught her eye. It was called Pot's From The Potteries, but there was not a single pot in sight as far as Emilia could see. The thing that had caught her eye was a picture in the window. It was a framed photograph of the Statue Of Mow that she had been to see hours before. It had been photographed during what looked like a build up to a storm. The photographer had been able to capture the dark purple sky behind it whilst keeping the rocks and grass in sharp, colourful focus. As Emilia stared, she focused on the rocks and everything else around her seemed to go quiet. The more she stared the more it seemed that the only things that existed was the picture and her, everything else had dissolved from her vision and gone silent to her ears. She knew it was a fixed photograph, but it now appeared as though the purple sky was moving in front of her. It was starting to look more and more like purple smoke or vapour, exactly like the surroundings when the Man had confronted her before. It was drawing her in, as if she was hypnotised and could not draw away from it.

"Like the picture do you, dear?" a lady's voice spoke, breaking Emilia out of her trance.

She turned to face the direction of the voice. The shopkeeper had appeared, a short stout woman with a narrow face, pointed nose, and an aura that suggested she was not one to be messed with.

"Yes, it's," Emilia turned back to look at the picture, "interesting," was all she could manage.

"Why not come in and have a look properly?" the woman asked, she immediately turned and started walking back into the shop and Emilia felt compelled to follow.

The shop was small but filled to the brim with very little

room to move. As soon as the door closed behind Emilia it was as if the outside world could not penetrate the stacked shelves. It looked older on the inside than it did from outside the door, as if it had not been disturbed in a long time. The shelves were full of books, games, toys, and models. To Emilia it felt like the sort of trinket shop you would see at a seaside town selling anything and everything to get tourists in the door.

"Have you been open long?" Emilia asked, trying to make pleasant conversation.

"Long enough to see many changes around here dear," came the lady's reply. "We were open before the centre was and moved in here the day it opened. First shop in here we were and will probably be the last too."

Emilia could not help but wonder how she was so confident, the shop in no way seemed to be doing well in a business sense.

"Business is good then?" she asked, more out of astonishment than curiosity.

"Steady, dear, steady."

Emilia had reached what she assumed was the till area now, a glass cabinet filled with yet more trinkets ranging from toy cars and trucks to fridge magnets and pens.

"What is this place?" Emilia asked herself quietly.

The woman appeared to the right of the till, carrying the picture that had caught Emilia's eye in the window. "Here it is, dear," she said kindly. She laid the picture on the worktop and slid it across to Emilia. "It was taken by a local photographer, don't know when, but he did well to capture the storm building behind the Old Man didn't he?"

Emilia nodded; it was truly a wonderful picture.

"Don't know when it was taken, no date, but I do know the legends around the rocks and the hill."

Emilia looked up, "What legends?" The question fell out of her mouth before she could catch herself. Now she had asked it though, she was intrigued. Maybe she knows something that can help, she thought to herself.

"The legend of the Man Of Mow. The story goes that he was worshipped by the first villagers on the hill. That they built the folly as a memory to him and believed that he was protecting us from something else." The woman was looking deep into Emilia's eyes, Emilia felt transfixed by her gaze. She continued, "There are some who believed he was good, and some that he was evil. Legend has it that there are those who oppose him, and they are the ones protecting us."

Emilia scoffed; she could not help it, "Sorry, I just think the good and evil thing is so over done these days." She blushed, she could not admit that she knew more than this woman as this would be yet another person that would potentially thank her, and she did not want that.

Unfazed, the woman continued, "Whatever you believe, know this. That hill, and everything on it, is connected. The stone runs deep, and it doesn't match any other stone and it has held firm for thousands of years. Nobody really knows what that folly was built for. The pile of rocks you see here were not built; they were forged out of nothing. They do not fit with the surroundings; they do not belong. Ask yourself, why would they be here, hmmm?"

Emilia froze. She had listened to every word the lady had said, but the bit that caught her ear was the 'hmmm'. It was a simple sound, one that she herself had made on occasion. But today after what had happened on that hill by the rocks, it sounded like a hum.

"What do you think it all means?" Emilia asked, shaking herself back in to focus on the room.

The lady smiled a knowing smile, "I believe that nothing happens without a reason, and that there is no smoke without fire. There may be some truth to the tales, who knows." The lady relaxed and retracted from the table.

Until this moment Emilia had not noticed how far she was leaning over it. Emilia found herself relaxing a little too.

"You really believe in the Man?" Emilia asked.

The lady shrugged, "I don't not believe," she said in an unconvincing way.

"What does that mean?" Emilia asked.

"It means that I choose to not believe or disbelieve. I think people should be allowed to believe what they wish. I do think some of the things that have happened on that hill are odd though. Remember a couple of years ago? The top of the hill turned black overnight, and they blame kids setting campfires? Never seen a campfire stay in a large perfect circle before. Have you?"

For the first time since entering the shop Emilia wanted to leave, and quickly.

"Then there was that poor girl who got caught in it all, even though nobody said anything, stories spread you know." The lady winked and tapped her nose knowingly, "Supposedly she did things that we will never know or understand to help us."

Emilia was sure she was visibly sweating by this point; she could not speak or move no matter how hard she tried.

"Now, enough story telling. Do you want to buy the picture?" the lady asked, apparently switching into full sales mode now.

Emilia looked at it again, with all the talk of stories she had forgotten that was the reason they were talking in the first place.

"How much is it?" she asked, surprising herself.

"Five pounds for you dear, you seem to love it, so I'll give you the family discount," the lady smiled politely.

Emilia considered for a moment, then without realising what she was doing replied, "Ok, yes please."

The lady beamed at her.

A few minutes later Emilia was outside the shop again holding a bag with the picture in. It had been wrapped in brown paper and protected. As she walked away from the shop, Emilia shook her head. She felt fuzzy, almost confused, "Why did I just buy that?" she scolded herself out loud. She stopped and took a breath. Calming herself she looked at the time. "Annabelle," she only had five minutes to get to the other end of the centre. She ran.

Annabelle worked at a fashionable clothes shop. Her discount had been used lavishly by the girls since she had started working there. Emilia arrived just as Annabelle was walking out of the shop she worked at. In her haste, Emilia nearly ran straight into her in the doorway.

"Woah," Annabelle exclaimed. "Where's the fire gorgeous?" She reached out to hold Emilia up by the shoulders. Smiling sweetly, "This is a lovely surprise but what's the hurry?"

Emilia was red faced and panting, to Annabelle it would have looked as though something had terrified her. "I just," she managed to get out between breaths. "I just wanted, to surprise you," she stopped to take some more deep breaths. "I got here early, so went shopping, then got distracted. Lost track of time."

Emilia then pulled Annabelle into a hug; this was as much to stop herself falling over as a desire for a hug.

Annabelle reciprocated, "Well, this is a lovely surprise. What did you buy? Show me?"

"Can we go sit down and get a drink?" Emilia panted, the colour slowly returning to her cheeks.

"Sure," Annabelle smiled, she linked arms with Emilia holding her up a little, and the two girls headed off to find somewhere to chat.

They ended up in a small family pub, ordered some soft drinks and sat at a table in the corner of the room. Emilia had returned to her normal colour now and they had settled down to have a chat and a catch up.

"So, busy morning then?" Annabelle asked with a raised eyebrow.

"No not really," Emilia replied sheepishly, "I went for a walk, then came here." She had decided to keep the difficult conversation for later. "I went shopping and lost track of time. Which is why, instead of being all calm, cool, and collected when you finished work. I arrived like a flaming fireball of haste," she smiled.

"Well, it was still a lovely surprise. So, what did you buy?" Annabelle asked curiously.

Emilia shared her purchases, they both agreed that the clothes were perfect, and Emilia had done well with her finds.

"What's in that bag?" Annabelle asked, indicated the bag that contained the picture wrapped in brown paper.

"Something for the house," Emilia replied unconvincingly.

Annabelle folded her arms and looked at her quizzically.

"It was an impulse purchase from a shop I've never seen before. Pots From The Potteries?" Emilia stopped to see if there was any reaction from Annabelle, there was not so she continued. "It's a little trinket type shop, filled with all sorts of weird and wonderful things."

"So, what did you buy for your house that's weird and wonderful?" Annabelle asked, curiosity clearly getting the better of her now.

Emilia had no choice, she bent down and picked up the bag. Putting the wrapped picture on the table she slowly began to undo the wrapping, "It is silly, but it's also strangely beautiful I think."

"Get on with it," Annabelle interrupted impatiently.

Emilia finished unwrapping the picture facing her, so Annabelle could not see yet. Then after taking a deep breath, she turned it round so she could see. "It is a photograph of the Statue Of Mow," she braced herself for the questions and response.

Annabelle did not immediately say anything, then she grinned. "You silly girl. You were late because you were buying a framed picture of a pile of rocks named after someone who you hate being associated with?" she chuckled. Emilia did not see what was so amusing and frowned.

"Come on," Annabelle said, "you must find that amusing?" she was grinning widely now, clearly enjoying this.

Emilia smiled a false smile; she was not amused at all by what Annabelle was suggesting. "I guess so," she lied. "I thought it was nice and the lady selling it was weirdly charming, so I just bought it." This was partly true, but Emilia was reacting to Annabelle's reaction as much as anything else. "I think the picture is lovely, and the colours are beautiful."

The girls looked at the photo, then after a few moments Emilia put it away packing it up neatly in its paper and putting it back in the bag.

"So, you had a good day then?" Annabelle asked.

"Yes, not too bad, odd but not too bad. What about you?"

"What you mean odd? Mine was dull but I want to hear about yours," Annabelle leaned forward curiously.

Emilia sat back, trying to work out how much of the day she wanted to reveal at this stage. "I went for a walk, retraced my steps from my first day in the village. The day I met Simon and he showed me around and stuff."

"That's cute," Annabelle smiled, sitting back to sip her drink.

"Yeah, I figured it would help with some of the stuff I've been dealing with. Try and get some real closure if you know what I mean?"

"I do, but you said odd. What was odd about it?"

Emilia took a deep breath, "I retraced my steps to the Statue Of Mow, the one in the picture. When I got there, I felt like I was being watched, like something was going on." She paused to judge Annabelle's reaction. To her surprise there was not one, Annabelle just sat there waiting for more. Emilia continued, "I climbed over the fences to get closer to the rocks. As I did there was a loud humming or buzzing. It sounded and felt like there was an electric current flowing through the ground."

"That is odd," Annabelle interrupted putting her drink down. "What happened next? Did you see him again or something?"

"No, didn't see him. In fact, what did happen was unlike anything I experienced with him before."

"So, what did happen?" Annabelle asked, clearly getting a little impatient now.

"As I touched the rock, someone appeared. A girl," Emilia waited, she wanted to see if Annabelle reacted. Nothing. "She appeared out of nowhere and landed on me, we ended up in a heap on the floor."

Annabelle snorted as she took a drink, "You must have looked a right pair. What did she say? What did you do?"

"You seem very amused by this," Emilia said sternly, "it was stressful you know."

"Ok, I'm sorry," Annabelle said, straightening her face so as not to laugh anymore.

"When she got off of me, she told me her name was Eleanor Smith," Emilia glared at Annabelle.

"Am I meant to know that name?" Annabelle asked, confusion on her face.

"You tell me," Emilia responded, she wanted to push the issue now and find out what was going on.

Annabelle sat back, "Sorry, are you suggesting I do know her?" Folding her arms, Annabelle was getting defensive now and she did not appreciate the insinuation.

"Here is what I know," Emilia said, leaning forward and focusing on Annabelle. "She got interested in me when she knew that I was meeting a girl called Annabelle. She clearly knew you because as soon as she knew that you were my girlfriend her face, body language, and tone changed. She claimed that she was looking for Annabelle Granger, but she stuttered before the Granger part as if making it up on the spot. I also don't think Smith is her real last name, she did the same there too. So, Annabelle. Why would a girl change her tone and seemingly panic when she knew that you were my girlfriend and run away as soon as I confronted her about it? Explain that to me," Emilia sat back and folded her arms, waiting for the admission from Annabelle, and that to be the end of it.

Annabelle glared at her, "Are you finished?"

"Finished what?" Emilia asked, a little confused.

"Finished accusing me, finished creating some crazy fantasy in your own mind? Not everybody is out to get you or hurt you, Emilia. I get that the humming thing would have freaked you out and I support you completely but are you actually accusing me of knowing that girl?"

"Well, she seemed to know you," Emilia replied, getting flustered now.

"Did she? Did she say, 'I know Annabelle Jones'?"

"No, she didn't but."

"Exactly," Annabelle interrupted. "She was looking for someone called Annabelle, you bumped into each other I have no idea how and you scared her with your normal aggressive tone. Then with everything else that has been going on, you put two and two together, got six, and decided to accuse me of something that is utterly ludicrous," Annabelle was defiant now, staring Emilia down.

Emilia looked into Annabelle's eyes, the eyes that she had looked into many times over.

"That's right Emilia, look at me. Look into my eyes and tell me that I am lying. Tell me that I knew that crazy girl by the rocks. Tell me that I am hiding it from you," there were tears forming at the corner of Annabelle's eyes now.

Emilia looked, and immediately felt the truth. Annabelle knew nothing, "I'm, I'm sorry," she stuttered out, tears forming instantly and rolling down her cheeks.

"How many times will we have this type of conversation Emilia?" Annabelle asked, fighting back the tears herself. "You are amazing and have been through so much, but I can't keep fighting with you. I have promised you over and over that I am on your side. Completely. Without question. But you need to stop challenging me and let me work with you."

Emilia, crying full tears now, wiped her eyes, "I know, I'm sorry I just, this is driving me crazy all the attention and focus."

"What attention?" Annabelle cut her off, "Nobody said anything to you about what happened, the Man, me, the stuff on the hill, none of it. Nothing."

"I know," Emilia sniffed.

"You can't keep throwing that in and thinking it lets you off being such an evil person to people." She started to put her things away, "Emilia, I am going to give you some space to work out what it is you want and need. You call me when you are ready to talk, ok."

"Don't leave Annabelle, let's talk. I'm sorry," Emilia was begging now, she had realised that she had pushed too far.

"Why should I Emilia? You saw a girl that said they were looking for someone with the same name as me and you immediately think I am conspiring against you?" There was real anger and pain in Annabelle's voice and face now.

Emilia had nothing to say, she could not think of anything that would fix this, "All I can say is I'm sorry."

"I'm sorry too," Annabelle replied. "Now you need to work out what you want to do." With that Annabelle stood, "You're the best thing that has ever happened to me," she said through tears. "But I can't keep having this fight and being hurt over and over. So, when you are ready to change that, you know where I am," she turned to leave.

"Where are you going? You're staying at mine this week," Emilia pleaded.

"Not now I'm not, I'm going home. If you want me, call me. But only when you are ready to be a grown up," that was the last thing Annabelle said before walking out of the door.

Emilia watched after her, speechless, tears rolling down her face. She felt as though her entire world had just left through the same door. As if everything had come crashing down around her in one go. There she sat, thinking about what to do next. All she could think of was how to win Annabelle back, and find out who that girl on the hill was.

CHAPTER 7

Ellie.

Ellie started to run, tears streaming down her face now. She had never met someone that got so mean and aggressive so quickly. All she wanted to do was put as much distance between her, the rocks, and that girl as she could, then sit down to try and work out what to do next. After a few minutes she had decided that she was not being followed, so she stopped to sit on a small rock and catch her breath. She looked around, the weather seemed the same and the time of day certainly seemed to match when she first made it to the Statue Of Mow. "What is going on?" she asked out loud, "What are you up to?"

Ellie decided that the best thing she could do was go home, get ready, and then go to surprise Annabelle as she had planned. Then the two of them could sit down together and work out what to do next. After catching her breath, Ellie stood and walked along the path back towards her house. It was a steady walk, but Ellie felt in a daze as if the world was passing her by without her really paying it much attention. Everything seemed normal, everything except the girl on the hill, that was the only thing that seemed out of place. She needed to find answers, but first she needed to relax and deal with one thing at a time.

A short while later, Ellie had made it home. Walking in the front door the first thing that she did was look around downstairs. Everything was exactly as she left it, even down to the breakfast dishes in the sink waiting to be cleaned.

She made herself a drink of juice and decided to go and get changed. She climbed the two flights of stairs into her third-floor bedroom and sat on the end of the bed. Ellie took a deep breath and closed her eyes to focus and think. After a minute or two she stood again and turned to get some fresh clothes, as she did so she noticed something on her bedside table. Crossing over to it, she picked up the picture of her and Annabelle. It had been taken last Christmas and they were both there laughing in their Christmas jumpers. Or rather, Annabelle was in the picture, but the girl she was with was not Ellie. Ellie stared at it, clutching it tighter and tighter. The girl in the picture was the one from the top of the hill. Emilia, Emilia Fields. Ellie put the picture back and started to tremble with fear. She looked round the room, it was her room filled with her stuff, but every little touch had changed to have Emilia instead of her. She ran from the room down the stairs, looking at pictures on the wall in the hallway, they had Emilia in. When she got to the living room it was Emilia in the school photos. The children's drawings on the fridge had been signed by Emilia. Ellie stopped and put her head in her hands, her head was spinning now. What had he done? Had he erased her from existence? Replaced her with someone else? She wracked her brain to try and figure it out, but she could not. She was in too much shock and could not focus. Without thinking, she turned and fled out of the house, Ellie knew she needed to get away. But to where? If she did not exist, where could she go? Who would listen to her and help her? Ellie took out her phone and unlocked it, her fingers froze though, unsure of what to do next. Who could she call? Looking back at her from the screen was Annabelle's beaming smile. Annabelle. If anyone could help her, she could. Even if she could not she would help Ellie figure out what to do next and support her. Deciding that she did not have much of a choice, Ellie headed for the bus that would take her to Annabelle's house.

"If Annabelle doesn't recognise me, I'm really lost," Ellie muttered to herself miserably as she hurried towards the bus stop. She immediately scolded herself, she had to stay positive as her mood was all she could currently control.

The bus journey seemed to take an age. Ellie had never wanted to get somewhere as quickly as she wanted to get to Annabelle's and as such every traffic light and stop at a junction seemed to last hours. Ellie was doing her best to stay in control, but it was not easy. When she eventually got off the bus, she ran to Annabelle's house so quickly and in such a blur that she did not remember doing it by the time she had arrived. She stopped at the top of Annabelle's driveway. Bending down with her hands on her knees she stopped to catch her breath. Ellie knew that turning up with red cheeks, puffy eyes, and panting as if she had just run a marathon would not send the best 'help me' message. The house, like her own, looked exactly as she remembered it. After a few moments, Ellie gathered herself and walked down the drive where the absence of her father's car reminded Ellie that Annabelle's parents were away. Ellie approached the door and rang the bell. Nothing. She knocked firmly on the door, still nothing.

"Come on Annabelle," Ellie begged out loud.

She took a step back and looked up at the windows, then moved to the right to peer into the living room. No sign of life anywhere. She turned away from the house, closed her eyes and focused her mind again. Before all the stuff at the pile of rocks happened, what was today's plan?

Then realization hit Ellie like a hammer, "You're at work. I was coming to surprise you!"

Ellie looked at her watch, Annabelle finished in just over an hour and there was not enough time for her to make it there. Ellie concluded that she would have to wait for her to come home, then her heart sank. She would not come home – Annabelle was supposed to be staying with Ellie this week, but now she would be staying with that vile Emilia girl. It was too much. Ellie had tears streaming down her cheeks at the realization that in one afternoon her entire world had come crashing down. She was tired, hungry, thirsty, and most importantly, alone. Alone in a world that she no longer belonged in, and if nobody knew or believed her how could she fix it? Ellie sat down on the doorstep outside Annabelle's front door, put her head in her hands and sobbed. In the space of a day Ellie had gone from the highest points of happiness to the lowest valleys of despair. She let it all out, and after a few minutes, looked up from behind her hands at Annabelle's driveway. She was not really looking at it, more just staring into space, wondering and thinking what to do. What was his plan?

"What are you up to?" she asked herself.

Ellie sat, pondered, and waited. She had decided that the next best thing to do was wait here to see if Annabelle did come home, if she did not then she would need to think of something else. Her only hope was that something else was different and had changed that meant Annabelle would be home instead of Emilia's. This meant waiting, waiting for at least two hours as she would need to allow enough time for Annabelle to finish and then make it home. Ellie was cold and alone, but also determined to work out what was happening and how to beat it. Beat the Man.

Ellie sat, occasionally stood and moved around a little to stretch her legs, but otherwise stayed close to Annabelle's front door. She checked her watch; she had been there for nearly two and a half hours. Besides needing the toilet, she was also very hungry and thirsty. With a final deep breath, she stood and started to head up the driveway resigned to the fact that Annabelle would not be coming home and so she needed to think of something else. She reached the top of the driveway and turned to head along the road and immediately stopped in her tracks. Standing right in front of her, a look of curiosity on her face, was Annabelle. Instinctively Ellie ran over and wrapped Annabelle in a tight hug, she buried her head in her shoulder and wept tears of joy.

"It's so good to see you," Ellie said as she pulled away. But to her horror, Annabelle had a look of confusion on her face.

"Do I know you?" Annabelle asked, pulling back a little in fear.

Ellie was instantly sent back to despair and shock in a matter of seconds.

"Annabelle it's me, Ellie."

Tears formed once more in the corner of Ellie's eyes.

"Are you the girl from the hill? The girl that Emilia was telling me about. The one that was looking for a girl named Annabelle?"

Ellie processed this; it was a lot of questions to field at once. "Yes, yes, and yes," she said finally. "I don't know what is going on, but I promise I just need to talk, I need your help."

Annabelle went to move past and head home, "I don't know you, and you are putting my relationship at risk so please just go."

She moved passed Ellie, confusion etched on her face.

"Ok, you don't know me! But I know you," Ellie called in desperation.

Annabelle stopped, but did not turn.

"I know you as well as Emilia does, maybe even better," Ellie was pushing it, and she knew it, but she had to try. "All I want to do is talk, because I need your help and if I'm right you are the only person I can trust."

Annabelle turned, "Prove it, prove that you know me," she folded her arms defiantly. "Emilia already thinks I have lied to her, so I may as well prove her right. So, prove to me you know me, tell me something only someone really special to me would know."

Ellie looked at her, focusing on her eyes. She needed to tell her something that would prove she was telling the truth, but not freak her out at the same time. "Ok, you once told me that in primary school you were teased about wearing glasses, so you used to take them off and squint at the back of the class, giving you headaches."

"Lots of people with glasses go through that, something else," came the cold reply from Annabelle.

Ellie was heartbroken, she had never seen Annabelle so cold and confrontational. "Ok, your biggest fears are wasps and spiders, you will run a mile if one goes near you or catches you by surprise."

Annabelle raised her eyebrow.

She wants more? Ellie thought to herself. "Fine. I tried to keep this sensible, but you give me no choice. You are ticklish on your right foot, your left shoulder, and the back of your neck.

You like walking in the rain and getting soaked. You will do anything for your friends, for me, they will always come first. We tease Simon about Sophie, about how they are soppy about being apart when at times we drive each other crazy. You like to link arms, but only on your left. You share your food with me, but only..."

"If I can have the first bite," Annabelle finished for her.

Ellie breathed a sigh of relief and smiled.

Annabelle softened, unfolding her arms, "I don't know who you are, but only Emilia knows some of that."

There was a pause, a silence between the two girls. Ellie decided to break it first, "Annabelle. I'm not trying to scare you or make anything difficult. I just need your help; I just need to talk. Please, can you just let me tell you what I know and then you can kick me out onto the street."

Annabelle opened her mouth to reply, then closed it again as if the words were stuck in her throat unable to form. After a few moments she finally spoke, "Ok, you can come in. I will give you an hour to talk to me, after that if I decide that this is all crazy you promise to leave me and Emilia alone?"

Ellie nodded, "Yes, I promise."

"Come on then," Annabelle turned and headed down her driveway.

Ellie smiled and did a little skip, this was the first bit of good news she had had since her time on the hill, but she knew she needed to make it count. She had one hour to convince Annabelle that she was not crazy and to help her against the Man, and whatever he was up to. Ellie followed Annabelle into the house, looking round it was the same situation as her own house. It looked the same, but she knew that any reference to her would have been replaced with Emilia.

"Would you like a drink?" Annabelle asked politely.

"Tea please, and can I just use your toilet as well? It's been a long day," Ellie asked, almost pleading.

"Sure, its-"

"Down the hall to the right, I know," Ellie smiled. Then immediately regretted it. She had hoped that little things like this would ease Annabelle but judging by her facial expression it simply made her more confused. "Sorry, I'll explain in a moment."

Ellie left and headed to the toilet. After she had sorted herself, she spent a moment looking into the mirror, staring at herself trying to focus her mind to create a plan of attack for the next hour.

"Come on Ellie," she said to herself. "Focus on the facts of what happened, tell her the story of the barbecue, and the walk over the hill and how you had planned to surprise her. Go from there and see what happens." With a last splash of water on her face she headed back to the kitchen where Annabelle was waiting with a suspicious look on her face.

Annabelle nodded at the chair opposite her, "Tea," she smiled as Ellie approached.

Ellie returned the smile and sat down. This was an unusual experience as she had never sat opposite Annabelle like this before, they had always been next to each other. She focused.

"Ok, I have been trying to work out the best way to try and explain, so I'm going to go to the beginning just to confirm a few things, then I'll fast forward to now. That ok?"

Annabelle nodded, "Go on," she said softly, sipping her own tea as she did so.

"Am I right that a couple of years ago, Emilia did something brave on the hill? Did she face off against the Man Of Mow to save our world?" she looked at Annabelle.

"Yes, she did," came the matter of fact style reply.

"And on that night, she banished him from our world to his between worlds prison?"

"I believe so yes, that is what she told me."

"Since then, you have been a couple yes? That was the night you first kissed?"

Annabelle flushed a light shade of red and nodded.

"I am also assuming that since then, even though you did your best to keep it a secret, people know and there is always something bugging Emilia. A constant pressure of thanks that irritates you both?"

"I think irritates is being very mild, it drives her crazy actually. In fact, it's the reason I am not with her now, she is concentrating on all the wrong things and-" she stopped. "Why am I telling you that? Sorry, please carry on."

Ellie paused, without knowing it Annabelle had started to sound like the Annabelle she knew and loved. She smiled, "Right, ok, thank you. That means that I think I am right. Here's the thing, Annabelle. I did all that too," she stopped, waiting for a response or a reply, anything. But there was nothing. "Where I am from, it was me that did all that stuff, me that caught the Man and me that, forgive the cheese, got the girl." This time Ellie flushed pink, "Then something happened." She continued, "This weekend we had a barbecue and I was complaining that I wasn't keen on the constant thanks and pressure. We, I mean, Annabelle and I had a small argument and she told me that I needed to calm down and focus on the positive stuff between us. Do you remember anything like that?" Ellie was hoping that she was on the right path here.

"Close, go on," Annabelle seemed to be letting her barriers down a little now, so Ellie pushed on.

"I agreed that I needed to just go with it, and let people say and think whatever they wanted to. Coming to today, I had decided to surprise you by coming to your work. I had some time to kill so I was retracing my steps around the folly, remembering when I first met Simon and how he had told me about the folly and the Statue Of Mow and stuff. I walked round to the rocks; you know the ones?"

Annabelle nodded, she also leaned in a little, clearly keen on what was being said.

Ellie continued, starting to gain a little confidence in what she was saying, and in the fact that Annabelle was at least listening to her. "Well, as I got close to the rocks, I heard a humming, a sort of buzz that got louder as I got closer."

Annabelle raised an eyebrow at this, Ellie continued taking it as a sign that she was matching this with what Emilia had told her.

"I got closer and when I touched the rocks I got pulled into his world, the Man's world. Whilst I was in there, he told me about time, he explained that he was going to make a change that would give him the upper hand, and help him win over me." Ellie paused, but Annabelle was still focussed so she continued, "He did something to me, he pulled my spirit energy out of me and split it, he called it a splice. He gave half back to me and half back into the timeline saying that change would lead him to victory. Then, he sent me back to the time of the first council. I saw it all Annabelle, the first council, the stones, all of it. Then, I went back to the rocks and touched them again I came flying back to now. That's when I landed on Emilia and she almost attacked me. I think," she stopped, this was the tricky part and she knew it, "I think the change he made was to replace me with Emilia but not kill me, just replace me in everyone's mind and then make me suffer through watching it." Ellie stopped. She had said all she could say and now she needed to just wait for Annabelle's reaction. Annabelle sat back, rested her hands on the table and exhaled deeply.

For a moment, neither of them spoke, Ellie knew this was a critical time and she needed to tread carefully for the next few moments. After what felt like an eternity, Annabelle spoke.

"You do know how crazy all that sounds?" she asked, looking up at Ellie as she did so.

Ellie responded with a nod, looking into Annabelle's eyes as she did so.

"Suggesting that Emilia, the girl I have known for years was created from a part of you, is insane," she looked out of the window, not at anything specific but just to the distance. "Crazy is what we do around here though isn't it? Ever since all the stuff with the council, the Man, all of it," she closed her eyes, a tear forming as she did so, "I think, I believe you," she said with a small quake to her voice. She lowered her head as if ashamed of what she was saying.

Ellie, a small wave of relief passing through her body, breathed calmly for the first time in a while, "Thank you," was all she could manage immediately.

Annabelle tutted at herself, "What do I do now? I've just told someone that I've never met, who apparently knows me better than anyone else, that I believe her over the girl I thought I knew? How do I even begin to deal with that?" she burst into tears and put her head in her hands.

Ellie got up and moved round the table to sit by

Annabelle, putting an arm around her as she did so. At first, Annabelle flinched, then relaxed and snuggled herself into Ellie's cuddle. For the two girls this was an unusual experience. Ellie was experiencing relief and comfort that for the moment at least she had Annabelle back. Annabelle on the other hand was feeling a sense of guilt for betraying Emilia, and confusion for not knowing how to deal with the situation.

"We will do it the way we always do," Ellie said eventually. "Together. That's what we do, we are a team, and we can beat anything together."

"That's easy for you to say," Annabelle retorted, a level of resistance in her voice. "I am the one who is taking the risk and betraying what I should believe in and follow. I can't even explain why it does, but even this now feels right. There is something that I can't see but I can feel that makes me believe you Ellie." Annabelle pulled away and turned to face Ellie once more. Looking deep into her eyes she said with a pleading tone to her voice, "You promise me that this is real, and that we are doing the right thing? Promise me Ellie."

Ellie took both of Annabelle's hands in hers, "I promise. I promise I am going to do what I can to fix this, but to do that I need your help. Probably Emilia's, Simon's, Leo's, all of them to make this right. I promise I am not here to hurt anyone; I just want my own life back."

The two girls looked at each other, holding hands and saying nothing.

"Can we eat now though?" Ellie asked. This broke the silence and mood at once, both girls chuckled and then the air was immediately cleared once more.

"Sure, I'll sort something," Annabelle replied and headed to the main kitchen area to sort out some food for them both. "Mum and dad are away, you can stay here and keep a low profile whilst we work out what to do, that ok?"

"Yes, I'll do what you think is best. I can't thank you enough Annabelle."

"Don't thank me yet, we need to work out what to do and then work out how to get everyone to help us. First though, most importantly, pizza or Chinese?" she asked with a smile.

Later after the girls had eaten a pizza from the local delivery, they were sat on the sofa in the living room. Annabelle had sent a message to Emilia saying she was home and that she just needed some time so to leave her in peace. They knew they needed to talk to Emilia, but not yet. For Ellie this felt like old times, eating, chatting, and drinking tea putting the world to rights was what they did best. She knew deep down though that this was not her Annabelle, or at least in memory it was not. They needed a plan.

"Do you still have some of that big flip paper around?" Ellie asked, "Feel that writing some of this down may help us is all."

"I think dad still has some around," Annabelle replied and went to look. A few moments later she was back holding a large pad of paper and some marker pens, "Emilia likes to draw her plans out too," she said calmly.

"Maybe we are the same then," Ellie replied with a smile, taking the pens as Annabelle laid out the pad on the floor. She knelt and drew a line across the sheet from left to right. "I want to try and recreate the images he showed me, when he had me trapped," she said, still looking down at the page. "This is the timeline," she stated.

Next Ellie added some circles, one at the end on the right then two close together towards the left-hand side of the line making three in total. She then numbered these one to three and added a dotted line after the one on the right, number three.

Sitting back, she began to explain, "Ok, number three is now, the moment that he trapped me and did whatever he did," she added '3 – *Splice*' to the bottom right of the page, like a key on a map. "Number two is the moment I was born," '2 – *Born*' was added to the key as she spoke. "One is where he made a change, whatever it was, to me that did whatever it did," '1 – *Change*' completed the list.

"What's the dotted line?" Annabelle asked.

"That's everything that hasn't happened yet, everything that happened after I bumped into Emilia on the top of the hill." Annabelle nodded in understanding.

"He was very clear with me that the change he made would not change anything I had already done but would change what happened next," Ellie mused, adding notes to the page as she did so.

"What do you mean next? Is he back?"

"I don't think he ever left. Kind of get the feeling he has been ahead of me, us, the whole time somehow. I don't think he planned to lose to us years ago, but he had a plan just in case," Ellie concluded. She had been adding to the page the whole time she was talking. The page was now full of notes detailing what Ellie had seen and experienced whilst in the vision. She had listed everything from the Abijah chant through to the Man appearing on the hill before the first council.

"That's a lot of detail," Annabelle said with a tone of admiration, looking across the page taking it all in.

"It's all I can remember. Annabelle, this is going to sound odd, but to you do I look or sound like Emilia?"

Annabelle looked up, confusion on her face, "You are very similar I guess, same height and face I suppose. You appear different, but you are very similar yes. As for sounding like her, your voice does a little. Why?" her eyes narrowed a little at this.

"Just trying to work out what he changed is all. What he did that makes him think he can finally get what he wants," Ellie tapped her chin with the pen, clearly thinking her way through the problem. "What do you want?" she muttered.

"Maybe he is messing with us?" Annabelle offered, "He has done it before, at least I assume he has to you? Did he appear to you twice as well, trying to get you to do the same thing but in different ways? Maybe it is the same thing?"

Ellie nodded, "Maybe. He was very confident that whatever he has done will mean he wins, and that he can grab all the energy from our world destroying it and pulling it into Imaginari," she sat back on the sofa, exhausted, she rubbed her face in frustration, "This is infuriating! I can't believe he has got in my head again."

Annabelle moved to sit by Ellie, this was the first time she had actively moved towards Ellie and it was comforting. She put her arm around her.

"We will figure it out," Annabelle said soothingly. "We did before, and we will again."

Ellie smiled, "Thank you. Thank you so much for listening to me."

"You're welcome. Now, I have an idea," Annabelle smiled.

Ellie raised an eyebrow, "I'm listening."

"It's late, and this is a lot to deal with, so, why don't you make yourself at home in the spare room. Then tomorrow I will see if I can get the others round to come and talk this through. What do you think?"

Ellie considered this. It was late, and she did need sleep, "Ok, but can we try and talk to Simon first, after you he is the person I trust the most and I think we may have a shot with Emilia if we get him on board?"

"Ok, Simon first, I am meeting the others tomorrow anyway, but I will do my best to talk to him alone if I can. Tyler won't be there; he is on holiday at the moment," Annabelle comforted, holding Ellie's hand as she did so.

"That's ok, we have a plan," Ellie said with a grin.

The two girls smiled warmly at each other, then shortly after went to get ready for bed, Ellie in the spare room and Annabelle in her own. Once she was alone, Ellie pondered everything that had happened today. She had gone through every emotion she thought possible and had still managed to end the day feeling positive. Annabelle had that effect on her, could always make every grey clouds silver lining shine through. Ellie did not know what would happen next, but what she did know was she needed to convince Simon to help. She needed to tread carefully and work out her moves with a clear plan. Annabelle would help and together they would figure it out. With these positive thoughts going through her mind, it did not take long for Ellie to drift into a deep sleep.

CHAPTER 8

Emilia.

Emilia sat motionless for a long time. She did not eat, drink, or even attempt to move. All she could do was think about what had just happened staring longingly out of the window, hoping that Annabelle would come back. She did not. Eventually Emilia was asked to leave as the coffee shop was closing for the night, initially she wanted to argue but the fight left her before she could open her mouth to speak. She left the coffee shop and headed out of the shopping centre towards the bus stop to go home. The thought of going home alone without Annabelle, especially after what had just happened, broke Emilia's heart. She did not know what to do, she felt lost as if nothing mattered. When she arrived at the bus stop, she realised she had gotten there on autopilot and could not really remember any of the walk to get there. She sat down on the seat in the bus shelter and waited. The bus was due in a matter of minutes, but it seemed like an eternity to Emilia. She took her phone out of her pocket and went to call Annabelle, then stopped herself. Annabelle's last words to her about being a grown up rang in her ears and she could not do it, she needed to wait until she was thinking clearly. All she could think of right now was Eleanor, the girl on the hill that as far as Emilia was concerned was responsible for all the negativity at the moment. She needed to find her, find out who she was and figure out a way to deal with it. The bus arrived, and despite the fact it was empty Emilia still moved to the back of the bus to be alone. She sat on the window seat and stared out at the passing streets as the bus moved through the town. As the bus journeyed out from the town into the surrounding areas it started to rain, the sort of rain that bounced off the floor and turned the sky black. The rain kept coming and when it was time for her to get off the bus she decided to run. As she ran along the street towards her home, she stopped and looked up at the folly once more. She looked but could not see it due to the rain. Defiantly Emilia shouted, "I know you have something to do with this." She stood in the rain for a moment as if waiting for a reply. Of course, there was not one, so she decided to carry on home. When Emilia made it home she was the first one there as her parents were still at work, she took advantage of this by quickly making herself a sandwich and a cup of tea. She then took her food upstairs and got out of her wet clothes and into her pyjamas. She dried her hair as best she could and then sat at her window seat looking at the rain falling against it. It had calmed a little now but was still heavy for the time of year. "To think we had a barbecue a couple of days ago," Emilia mused to herself. She ate her sandwich, and as she was sipping her tea, she heard her phone vibrate with a text message, it was from Annabelle.

Emilia, I have made it home ok and I hope you did as well. I think we need some time to think, so let's chat tomorrow and go from there. A x

Emilia read the message twice over, to make sure she was reading it right. She then slammed the phone down on the floor in anger and immediately felt her blood begin to boil.
"How can she say that? How can she want to be away from me? Surely we should talk about this?" she said angrily to the empty room. "Fine, have it your way. I'll leave you in peace and then we shall see what everyone thinks tomorrow shall we."
She turned back to the window and looked up at where the folly should be, it was just visible now but was still obscured by rain and clouds. She was angry, but as that faded away it turned to sadness and fear. Had she lost everything? Was her

world falling apart? Emilia's emotions and feelings morphed into resilience and defiance. She would not be beaten nor torn apart by this, she would show resolve and fight for what was hers. Emilia watched the rain as it settled down and calmed to nothing, the wind still blew strong but otherwise it turned to a clear night. She had not heard from her parents, nor did she want to. Eventually she decided it was time to go to bed. Turning out her light with one last look up the hill, she settled down and soon drifted off to a deep dreamless sleep.

Emilia woke early the next day and immediately her mind drifted towards the situation she was in. She lay in bed, trying to stay calm and focused before getting carried away with the day. It worked to a point, one of the benefits of her room was that she could stay hidden as if still asleep whilst her parents got ready for work. Laying there listening to the hustle and bustle downstairs. She heard showers being used, the clatter of kitchen ware, and general movement. Eventually she heard the front door open and close, followed by the sound of two people walking on the driveway, opening car doors, and then driving away. Peace and quiet, the house to herself, just what she needed and wanted. It was just before nine and Emilia was meeting up with Simon, Leo, Dan, and Annabelle by the canal at around twelve, so she had plenty of time to relax, gather her thoughts and prepare for the day. From her bed she could see the clear sky out of the window, the rain clouds had gone, the day seemed to be warm and dry with white wisps of clouds.

"Canal path will be muddy though," she commented to herself.

Emilia created a mental plan for the day, she needed to keep structured to stay calm and focused to get through it all. She spoke out loud to herself as she planned.

"One, send a text to Annabelle saying morning and hope you slept well, also comment that you are looking forward to seeing her. Two, get washed and have some breakfast," she was counting on her fingers as she did this, Emilia felt it helped her remember everything if it was numerical. "Three, get ready for the day, thinking jeans and a top with decent trainers. Four, meet them all, talk to them all, and hope that Annabelle comes and plays along. Five, depending on how four goes, see what everyone thinks about Eleanor," There was a tone to her voice as she said that name, she could not help it. "Ok, Emilia, that seems like a good plan now get up and do step one," she sat up in bed and reached for her phone. She had no new messages or anything, so she went to send a text to Annabelle.

Morning. How'd you sleep? Just wanted to say hi and say that I'm looking forward to seeing you later. Hopefully we can talk, and we can get back on track. You know what I'm like! See you later – E x

Emilia read the message to herself a few times to make sure she was happy then pressed send, immediately feeling a little better. Next on the list was to get washed and have some food, so Emilia moved to the bathroom to have a shower. A little while later she was sat in the kitchen in her dressing gown, hair wrapped in a towel eating some cereal. Cereal was not Emilia's first choice, but she did not have the energy or desire to make a cooked breakfast for one person. After eating, Emilia did the washing up including her parent's dishes and mugs, then went upstairs to get ready. She checked her phone, no reply from Annabelle but there were messages in the group chats that had confirmed everyone was still meeting up today as agreed. Emilia felt a little annoyed that Annabelle had not replied, but she had not replied to the group either so that calmed her a little. Emilia got herself dressed and sat at her table to do her hair and makeup. She did not want to do a lot and look over dressed, but enough to look presentable. After getting ready, Emilia sat in the living room, she had her bag ready to go with the essentials and a coat just in case it decided to rain again. This was England in the summer after all. She looked at her watch, it was just before eleven and after checking the weather and she decided to leave early and walk down the hill to the canal, then along it to the pub they were all meeting at for a drink. She had decided that the fresh air would probably do her some good, so she set off. It was in fact a pleasant day, other than a few puddles on the floor and some damp roads, it was a perfect summers day. Emilia had to carry her coat as it was too hot to wear it. After following the road for a short distance, she was soon crossing the fields heading towards the canal. This was one of the things that Emilia liked the most about the village she called home, there were not really many big walks, but hundreds of short ones that could be bolted together to make up a walk of almost any length to get anywhere you wanted to be. On this route, Emilia could see the folly behind her up on the hill and the wide-open spaces of the fields ahead of her. The fresh air was helping, Emilia just walked and listened to the sound of countryside as she did so, and it cleared her head completely of any negativity or anger. She walked through the fields, through a small wooded area, under a railway bridge and down to the canal. Once at the canal she turned left and headed along it in the direction of the pub. It was a hot day, Emilia was drinking her water at regular intervals and doing her best to stay in the shade as she walked by the water. Emilia liked this part of where she lived, it was close enough to be near the essential things like shops but remote enough to be quiet. She only saw a small number of people whilst she walked on the canal. A cyclist who came up from behind so quickly that she needed to leap out of the way before getting run down. A girl who she had not seen before, a very friendly girl who had an even friendlier black-haired labradoodle with her. She stopped to fuss the dog and exchanged pleasantries with the girl. Apparently, she lived nearby but also enjoyed the solitude of the village. Before long, Emilia had made it to the join between two canals, she went down the steps and could finally see the place where she was going to meet her friends. It was nearly twelve and as she had anticipated, she was the first to arrive. There were a few other groups already sat at some of the tables outside by the canal. She went inside to get herself a drink. Emilia had been to the Brown Dog pub a few times this summer, mainly for food with family and occasionally with friends. It was the sort of place that was warm and welcoming, the sort of place that locals loved, and tourists enjoyed. She ordered a blackcurrant and lemonade as well as a pint of water, she had worked up quite a thirst on her walk. She went back outside and claimed a table near the water's edge, it was a glorious day and all traces of the previous night's rain had now disappeared. Emilia did not have to wait long, shortly after she had sat down Leo and Dan arrived, they walked down the road and into the driveway. She waved to them, Leo waved back and called out to her.

"Just going to get a drink, be there in a sec."

Emilia nodded in understanding and smiled to herself, the fact that they had arrived first would hopefully make this easier.

A few moments later the boys had joined her with their drinks and after exchanging hugs, sat down. Leo to her left and Dan opposite her on the bench.

"So, what's new then boys?" she asked, eager to start a conversation and she did not want to start off with her complex one.

"Not much," Dan replied first. "Work and getting ready for university for me. Dull."

"Same, but less of the work," came Leo's response. He had been doing more work with his parents and so had not had time to get a part time job like the others.

"Well, aren't we living the teenage dream?" Emilia joked, raising her glass. "To teenage dreams."

The boys raised their glasses and the three clinked them together and laughed. The conversation moved on, and shortly after Simon arrived.

"Not having too much fun without me I hope?" he teased as he walked over, holding his own drink of lemonade. He sat down next to Dan on the bench, "What did I miss? Where's Annabelle?" he asked looking at Emilia.

"Actually, that's a good question" Leo added.

All three boys were now looking at Emilia, and she knew she needed to say something to deal with this.

"How should I know?" was all she could think of on the spot, she knew she was looking guilty though and her tone was a giveaway.

They all stared at her, Simon said with a raised eyebrow, "I know that look Emilia, come on, out with it."

Emilia knew she had no choice but to start talking about where Annabelle was and what was on her mind, she took a breath to steady herself. "We had a row, I'm not convinced it wasn't over nothing, but she also made it worse. So, it's not all my fault despite what she may be saying or doing with that other girl." She had gone red and felt as though the lid had been lifted off the pot of her emotions and they were boiling over onto the table. "A lot has happened in the last twenty-four hours and I am learning a lot about what people really want and think, and anyone who thinks they can fool me will soon learn that I won't be so easy to trick."

Her three friends stared at her, astonished at the outburst of emotions and rage that had just happened. Eventually, Simon spoke first.

"Emilia, I think you need to take a breath and tell us exactly what happened? Then maybe we can help," he smiled kindly.

Emilia softened; she could not stay angry when Simon was around to help. As her best friend she trusted him explicitly and so conceded that she would need to tell them the whole story.

"Fine," Emilia said, taking a sip of her drink as she did so. "This is what happened yesterday. I was retracing my steps from the first time I went up the hill, the day I met you Simon, keeper of sweeties," she smiled at him, everyone chuckled, and she continued. "I walked round to the Statue Of Mow round the back of the hill. As I got closer, I felt like I was being watched, like there was someone there, I couldn't see anyone though. I got there and climbed over the barriers, wanted to get a closer look."

"Naughty," Leo interrupted. "Safety first Emilia." He nudged her with his elbow and winked.

"Oh shh," she retorted, pushing him back playfully. "As I got closer to the rocks there was a loud buzz, or hum. Kind of like static electricity or something. When I eventually got my hand to touch the rock there was a loud bang and this girl appeared out of nowhere and landed on top of me."

"Ok, then what?" Leo asked, they were all showing real interest now.

"I asked her who she was, what she was doing there and stuff," Emilia paused, she was aware this was the tricky part of the story to tell as deep down she knew how it would sound. It would sound as if she was crazy and jealous. After a deep breath, she continued, "She said her name was Eleanor Smith, that she lived in the village although I've never seen her before, and that she was looking for a girl named Annabelle, Annabelle Granger. After I confronted her a little she ran off, haven't seen her since."

"Ok," Simon commented, "I feel like there is an 'and then' end to this story?"

The boys nodded, and once again looked at Emilia.

"You're not wrong," she stated firmly. "I was going to surprise Annabelle when she finished work. Anyway, after I had got there, and we were having a drink, we got onto the subject of the folly and the Man and the rocks etc. She knows what I'm like, as do you guys, that I hate any conversation about it. Any kind of thanks or anything and I just get angry. In the heat of the moment, I asked if she knew an Eleanor, which she denied. Not only did she deny it, she immediately went on the defensive and blamed me when all I did was ask how a girl I've never seen before seemed to be looking for her. Not like Annabelle is a common name round here or anything is it? So, there you have it. That's what happened and why Annabelle is being so evasive."

Emilia drank the last bit of her drink and sat back, arms folded. She felt victorious, as though saying it out loud had helped deal with it. All she had to do now was wait for the agreement and the replies of support. They did not come. In fact, all that did happen right away was silence, complete and total silence amongst the four friends. The three boys looking at each other, then back to Emilia, clearly working out what to say. Most importantly, who was going to speak first. Dan shifted in his seat, as did Leo, then finally Simon spoke.

"Without sounding rude Emilia, is that it?" he asked, cautiously.

Emilia glared at him, "What do you mean, is that it?"

"Well, is that all that happened? Is that all that was said and stuff?" he asked, looking very uncomfortable as he did so.

Emilia's eyes narrowed, "Yes, Simon," she said coldly, "that is all that happened. Why?"

He tilted his head to one side and looked at her sympathetically, "Ok, you want me to be honest I assume, as always?" he asked, clearly showing signs of working out his next words as he spoke.

Emilia nodded, not taking her narrowed eyes off him as she did so.

"Well, it doesn't seem as though anything happened."

"What?" Emilia shouted, louder than she intended but she was not happy with this as a comment from him.

"I'm just saying that based on that, everything you just said, nothing happened. Certainly nothing to be this angry about. The weirdest thing is the fact this girl appeared out of nowhere. That is the only thing I can see that is worthy of this much attention? Guys, do you agree?"

He looked at Dan and Leo, clearly wanting support. They nodded sheepishly and muttered words of agreement but nothing with conviction.

He continued, "I get that this stuff freaks you out and angers you, I get that you don't want the attention, but this seems a little bit extreme on your part."

Emilia was ready to explode with rage, "You think this is normal? You think that I am making this up? You think that I want to argue, and find fault, and push people away? Is that it?" she was shouting now, and people from other tables were starting to look in the direction of the four friends.

"Ok, just listen to me, ok?" Simon softened his voice and leant in, trying to get Emilia to calm down. "Put the stuff about where she came from to one side. You said yourself you didn't recognise her, but that doesn't mean she isn't local does it? You don't know everyone do you?" he looked at Emilia, she glared back, so he carried on. "Knowing you as I do, you wouldn't have spoken to Annabelle about it you would have challenged her, and the moment she denied anything you would have pushed even harder. Am I right?"

He raised an eyebrow; he knew Emilia very well and she knew it.

Emilia said and did nothing.

"I'm taking that silence means, at the very least, I am not wrong. Look, I don't know who she is, where she came from, or if she knows our Annabelle or not. But what I do know is it is more probable that it's nothing. And the bit you should be focusing on is where she came from, not whether Annabelle knows her or not. You know what the Man did to you last time, if he is back, and if something is going down, then surely we need to understand it, not argue about it?" he sat back and smiled kindly.

Leo and Dan did the same, Emilia was now greeted by three kind looking faces all relaxed and concerned.

"Maybe," she said, a little more harshly than she intended. "I don't know. I just get so wound up by it all."

"We know," Leo said, "that is why Simon is right. We should talk and help each other, not argue about it and make it even more complicated than it needs to be." He put his arm around Emilia and she immediately relaxed a little. "Come on, calm down and let's talk. Annabelle will be here soon, and we don't want a row."

Emilia nodded; she knew they were right. In her heart she knew that it was most likely nothing, or at least something that Annabelle did not know about or had caused. She did get angry when it came to the Man and everything related to it. Was it possible that she had connected some dots, leapt to a conclusion, and then gone on a war path? If she was honest with herself, the answer was probably yes.

"Ok," she said, with a tone of acceptance. "What do we do now then?"

The boys smiled, "First, we get another drink. Then we talk about the mystery Eleanor who appeared from nowhere," Dan said. "I'll get these," he stood to go to the bar.

"I'll help," Emilia added, she wanted to move to shake off the anger and mood from herself.

After getting the drinks order, they both went inside to get the next round for everyone. Whilst in there, Emilia and Dan did not really speak, or rather, they did not speak about what had just happened. A few minutes later they emerged carrying two drinks each, as they approached the table though they realised they would need to go back in again.

"Work is killing me," Annabelle said, she had sat down next to Simon meaning she was diagonally across from where Emilia would be sat. Emilia and Dan approached and gave out the drinks they had.

"Hey Annabelle," Dan said with a smile.

"Hi," she replied beaming.

Emilia could not help but smile and feel comforted by that smile. "Hey," she said softly.

"Hey you," Annabelle replied sweetly, smiling at Emilia and giving her an extra bit of eye contact.

"Glad you could make it."

"Well yes! But you all started without me didn't you! I'm going to get a drink, then I want catching up on everything," she stood and headed away into the bar.

Emilia stood and hurried after her, she caught up with her just as she got to the door.

"Hey, can we talk for a minute?" she asked, the previous brief conversations had forced her to calm down and focus on the issues at hand.

"We can talk, but I don't want to be shouted at," Annabelle replied.

"Look, I just wanted to say I'm sorry, and I really want to try and make this work. I want to calm down and deal with things, and the truth is I can't do any of that without you. I need you Annabelle, and I'm sorry," she looked into Annabelle's brown eyes.

Annabelle looked back and said nothing at first. Then she smiled and pulled Emilia into a hug, kissing her on the cheek as she did so.

"It's fine, just remember that I am on your side and not everything is a fight or a confrontation with me. I won't always agree with you, but I am always on your side. Ok?"

Emilia nodded.

"Right, now let me get a drink so we can go and chat to the boys and see what's going on, ok?"

Emilia smiled, the girls let go of each other and whilst

Annabelle was at the bar Emilia headed back out to the table with the boys. She felt better, and all she needed to do was talk it out with her friends and make the most of the situation. There would be a solution, all she needed to do was find it and she could not do that alone.

After Annabelle returned, the conversations moved on. Emilia and the boys immediately moved the conversation away from the Man for now, even though they did not say it out loud, they were all thinking the same thing; that they did not need that conversation yet. They discussed work, plans for the next couple of weeks, and just about anything that came into their minds at the time. They ate, drank, and laughed for most of the afternoon. To Emilia this was exactly what she needed, friends, and time with them. After a couple of hours Simon gave Emilia a knowing nod, she knew that she needed to raise the subject about the rocks and Eleanor soon. The nod from Simon was his way of saying, *If you don't, I will.* Emilia waited for the right time to turn the conversation in that direction, the problem was that everyone was engrossed in talking about the upcoming football season and she knew there would not be an easy way to turn that conversation. As it turns out, she did not need to worry as someone else made that decision for her and raised the topic themselves.

"So, Emilia, are we going to talk about the Man and the fact that he is playing with your mind again?" Annabelle questioned out of the blue.

Emilia was stunned, she was at a loss for words and did not know how to respond. She had been so focused on working out how to bring it up that she had not considered what would happen if someone else did.

"Well, yesterday was strange," she stuttered out.

"I'll say," interrupted Annabelle. "How have you not mentioned the stuff that happened over the hill, by the rocks, and then the fact that you brought a picture of the Statue Of Mow on a whim?"

"She did tell us some of it," Leo stated, "but nothing to do with a picture."

They all turned to look at Emilia.

"Well, I didn't think that bit was important," she exclaimed.

"No, the bit we all want to talk about is the girl you saw on the hill," Simon added. "What do we think?"

Nobody said anything for a moment, then Emilia decided to act.

"Well, she appeared out of nowhere and seemed to know Annabelle. I know she clearly didn't," she added quickly, sensing that Annabelle and the others were ready to jump on her about that comment. "So, I am assuming that he is back and up to something, but I don't know what. I find it infuriating that he is out there again."

"I thought he was gone?" Dan asked innocently.

"So did I," Emilia agreed. "But maybe all we did was lock him away and wind him up for a couple of years?" she added with a sigh.

"So, seems to me that we only have one option," Simon added, they all looked at him. "Well it's obvious isn't it? The only person who can help us, the only one who can answer these questions. Is the girl on the hill, Eleanor? We need to find her, don't we?"

They all looked at each other, Emilia only looked at Annabelle to try and read her reaction, she could not as she was hiding behind her drink.

"Ok, seems sensible," Emilia agreed.

"How do we do that though? She could be anywhere," Leo added.

They all looked at Emilia.

"How do I know?" she defended strongly.

"You saw her, did she go anywhere? Say anything? Anything at all that may help us?" Dan enquired.

Emilia shook her head, "No, she just said Annabelle's name and then ran off."

"Actually, I can help," Annabelle said calmly.

They all looked at her with expressions that were a mix of surprise, intrigue, and in Emilia's case, anger.

"How?" she asked, trying to keep as calm as possible.

"Stay calm Emilia," Annabelle stated. "Let me get through this whole thing, ok?"

Emilia said nothing.

Annabelle continued, "After I left Emilia last night I went straight home. I was upset, angry even, at the argument we had. As I got home, I was met by a girl that matched the description of the one Emilia saw on top of the hill, she confronted me."

She paused, expecting more questions but none came, they were all drawn into what she was saying now.

"What happened next?" Emilia asked, her arms folded and with an anger to her tone. Emilia could feel her blood beginning to boil again and was fighting to keep control.

"She talked, she knew things, things about me, us," she gestured to the group. "Things that nobody could know without some serious digging. So, I listened to her."

"You listened to her?" Simon asked.

"Yes, as in I let her explain from her side what had happened."

"Tell us." Leo demanded, "That's the stuff we want to hear!"

"I can go one better," Annabelle replied, "you can ask her yourself; she is at my house right now."

Silence fell over the group. They were all astounded as to the situation they were in. Emilia was raging inside but was keeping quiet whilst she worked out what to say and do next.

"You are unbelievable," Simon said. "Why didn't you just lead with that or invite us all round earlier?"

"Because I wanted us to discuss it first," Annabelle replied with a smile.

"Well, I think we all need to go to yours, don't we?" Dan asked, finishing his drink, and looking to stand and move away.

"Do we?" Emilia interrupted coldly. They all looked at her, smiles fading. Emilia had turned scarlet with rage. "Let me just get this straight. I meet someone that claims to know you," she pointed at Annabelle accusingly. "You deny it, then storm away from me only to, as far as I can tell, spend the night with that very person chatting over tea as if it is perfectly normal? And you choose not to tell me and keep it a secret to then reveal it like some kind of hero? And you all agree to follow along and meet this girl and see why she is the sudden wonder star of the village?" Emilia stood, emotion taking full control now, "I cannot believe you, all of you."

"Emilia, wait, listen, you just agreed that talking to Eleanor is the best thing to do, why has that changed?" Simon asked, concern etched into his voice.

"Because, Simon," Emilia spat his name with fury. "That was before I knew that she had been trying to steal my girlfriend, before I knew that it had been kept hidden from me like I am some sort of child that cannot be trusted." She looked around, daring any of them to challenge her on this. The faces that greeted her were ones of fear and confusion. "So, let me ask you all a question. Do you want to go and meet this girl that Annabelle kept hidden from us, or come with me to find another way out of this mess?"

The looks changed to confusion.

"Emilia, the only thing to do is talk to her, wherever she is," Leo replied, a small amount of fear to his voice.

"Fine, that's how you all feel is it? In that case, I am leaving."

With that Emilia turned and stormed away over the small canal bridge and back the way she had come earlier that day.

"Emilia, wait," she heard Annabelle call.

She ignored her and quickened her pace to get away from the people that, as far as she was concerned, were betraying her. She had never felt so much fury and rage, and as she walked it seemed to get stronger and build up more pressure inside.

Emilia walked and walked. She missed the first turning to get back on the road from the canal and kept going, she was glaring up at the folly, standing on the hill where it always was with the pale blue sky all around it. She reached the second road bridge, exited the canal, and headed up the hill on the road into the village, all the time keeping one eye on the folly, for some reason she felt she needed to go there. She eventually arrived on the peak of the hill, sweating and still furious with her friends.

"How can they have turned on me?" she shouted. "Why did they betray me?"

She was alone on the hill so of course there was no reply.

"Come on, show yourself," she demanded to the stone folly.

Nothing. After a few moments Emilia stormed away towards the Statue Of Mow, in her mind the place where all this had begun. It did not take her long to get there. She climbed over the barrier once more and stopped to listen. No humming or buzzing, just the sound of the soft breeze in the trees.

"Are you here instead?" she demanded of the rocks. "Come out," she screamed as she stomped over to the rock face.

She slapped the nearest one with her palm and immediately regretted it. The stinging burning pain sent a shockwave up her arm.

"Ow," she shouted again and collapsed to her knees. Crying now, holding her wrist to try and stop the pain. She sobbed, bending forwards to bury her face in the soft damp grass.

"What do you want from me?" she mumbled into the ground. "I just want my life back, I'll do anything. Just tell me what you want."

There she stayed for a few moments, eventually sitting up revealing her tear-stained face and puffy eyes to the world. She looked at her palm, it was red and stinging but otherwise seemed ok, at least until she tried to shake it off. That hurt, and she grabbed hold of it again wincing as she did so.

"Now here is a sight I had been hoping for, and I must admit it has arrived sooner than I could have hoped," came a soft, soothing voice. "Who would have thought that Emilia Fields would ever be so miserable and alone. So alone, that she would come to me for help."

CHAPTER 9

Ellie.

Ellie slept well, in fact she slept right the way through to when Annabelle woke her with a cup of tea at around nine.
"Wakey wakey," came Annabelle's soft voice as she knocked on the door and peered round it.
Ellie sat up quickly, for a few moments a little disoriented as to where she was, then focused on Annabelle at the door.
"Yes, sorry slept longer than I wanted to," she said groggily.
"That's ok, figured you needed it," she replied as she entered the room offering the tea. "Also, assuming that you need your tea before you can do anything?" she added with a grin.
"Yes, you do know me after all," Ellie commented warmly. She sipped the tea, "Thank you again for last night, and letting me stay and, well, everything."
"You're welcome. We're going to need to be on it today to convince the others you know."
Ellie nodded, rubbing the sleep out of her eyes as she did so.
"Ok, I'll go and start some breakfast, you wake up a bit and come down when you're ready. That ok?"
Ellie nodded again, smiled, and then added, "Thank you."
Annabelle smiled, then stood and left, closing the door behind her.
Ellie sat in bed for a moment, sipping her tea whilst she thought about the day ahead. She needed to be sure of what was going to happen as best as she could. Ellie knew she needed to rely on Annabelle, hoping that she would be able to convince her friends to come and talk to her. Once that was

done, it was up to Ellie to convince them of the events that had unfolded. She sipped her tea, pondering, "First though, breakfast."

A few minutes later Ellie was downstairs with Annabelle who had made omelettes for breakfast.
"Smells good," Ellie commented as she entered the kitchen.
"My specialty," came the grinning reply as Annabelle put the food on plates and gave one to Ellie.
"Thanks," Ellie said gratefully.
The girls ate in near silence, other than the usual questions of how 'did you sleep' and offerings of more tea. Once they had eaten, Ellie was doing the washing up when she decided to chat about the day ahead.
"So, you ok talking to Simon and seeing if he will come back here to meet me?" she asked.
"Going to try," Annabelle replied between sips of juice. "We are all together, so if I have to do it all in one go then I will. I have a feeling that Emilia may beat me to the punch though, she won't be happy today and may bring up the subject of you before I get chance to talk to him."
"What do you think she will say?" Ellie asked nervously.
"No idea. She won't be happy that we argued last night, and that I denied knowing you only to then chat to you, let you stay over, and cook you breakfast." There was a tone to Annabelle's voice that suggested she was as nervous as Ellie. "Emilia can be hot headed at times and may not listen to reason," she concluded.
"Here's hoping today is not one of those days then."
"Indeed. Right, I'm going to get ready to go, you going to be ok here today? Just kill time and then I'll be back later with news, good or bad, cool?"
"Cool," Ellie said as she washed the last glass and turned to face Annabelle. "Thank you, again."
Annabelle smiled, and left the room to get ready to meet the others.

After Annabelle had left, Ellie made herself comfortable in the living room. She had the house to herself so may as well enjoy it while she could. Sat on the sofa with a cup of tea and some biscuits, she soon forgot about most things that were running through her mind. She turned the TV on for some background noise, instinctively she put it on a channel that would show her favourite shows on repeat all day, meaning she did not need to do anything and could just relax – exactly what she needed. Ellie was comfy, so comfy that before long she had snuggled down and drifted off to sleep.

Ellie found herself in her own house, she recognised the unique round window of her room. Everything appeared to be hers and as she remembered it, but there was a haze in the room. It was as if she was viewing everything from a great distance and it was blurred, even though she was in the room itself. Looking round, Ellie was comforted by the fact that the pictures in the room had her in, not Emilia, she went downstairs and was also satisfied that this was the case in every room of the house. Emilia was gone it seemed. Heading into the garden she went over to the stone key that had been so crucial years ago. It was still there, but unlike the usual stone, she could see the beams of light heading up to the folly. They were the same as the ones that the Man had shown her before, but she had never seen it like this, from this stone in her garden. The flow was moving up towards the folly just as she remembered it, but it was being drawn from all around it. The plants, grass, and trees were all sending beams of energy to the stone. Which it then appeared to be combining into one to send up to the folly.

"Makes sense I guess," Ellie commented. "The energy is supposedly from all living things in our world, makes sense that the stone would send it all up. But why didn't he show me that? He only showed me the single beam?" She moved closer. As she got near the stone, she knelt to get a closer look. She reached out her hand to touch it, and noticed that it was not only pulling energy from the living things in the garden, it was also pulling it from her. Very faint, but it was there, drawing the same beams of light from her as it was the plants. She stood, puzzled by this, and then walked round to stand in the way of the beam going towards the folly.

Nothing changed; it carried on flowing through her as it did before, as if she was not there at all. Ellie headed over to the tree in the garden, it was sending the biggest beam to the stone, Ellie presumed this was because it was the largest living thing in the garden. When she was in front of it, she leaned in to examine it closely, reaching out with her palm to touch the bark of the trunk. As she did, she noticed a faint vibration in her palm, she pulled it away and looked at it. There was nothing there, so she reached out once more. The same thing happened, a small vibration that was noticeable but not uncomfortable. Then Ellie realised that her hand seemed to be drawing the energy from the tree into it. There were multiple strands of light going into her palm and when Ellie looked closely, she noticed her hand was glowing slightly. She pulled it away and the strands of light broke and stopped going into her palm, then the vibration went away as did the glow. Ellie stared at her own hand, she also noticed that the graining from the stone Man Of Mow she had gotten earlier had gone, her hand was back to normal. Turning she bent down and put her hand against the grass where the same thing happened. Small vibrations, a glow to her palm and strands of light moving from the grass to her hand. Ellie did this on multiple things in the garden, everything that was living had the same effect. Anything that was not, like the stone itself, the patio, or the metal garden table did not react to her palm. "What is that all about?" she asked. Inside, it was the same story, pot plants did the same thing, even the fruit on the kitchen table gave off a little bit of light to her hand. She walked through the house, in the hallway noticing a glow around the front door, as if there was a bright light just the other side of it. She walked up to it and opened the door. Ellie could not see her driveway, the door had opened onto the hilltop by the folly, the bright light she had seen was the sun beating down from the clear blue sky. Shielding her eyes, she stepped through the door on to the grass of the hilltop and looked around. There she was alongside the folly on a clear day as if she had walked up there herself. Turning, the door she had come through had vanished, nowhere to be seen.

"Guess I'm walking home then," she commented.

On an impulse, she headed over to a large bush to see what would happen. To her amazement, the same thing happened but much stronger. The strands of light reached her before she could reach out her hand and she could see them reaching out to her whole body. Ellie felt like a magnet drawing metal filings to it, and it seemed to be that her body could absorb it and take it in. To what end she had no idea, nothing had ever happened that would suggest why this was the case, nor what it meant or was for.

"This is so strange," she said to herself as she moved away from the bush.

Looking up at the folly, she could see the beams of light from the five keys entering the building and then the largest one of all going up into the sky. She walked up to the folly and tried to see if the beams of light there would enter her palms. They would not.

"So, it only works for things where the energy has not gone into the stone keys yet," she commented, making a mental note of what she had seen.

Heading back down the steps to the hilltop from the folly, then turning to go down the hill to walk home, Ellie noticed that as she moved past the plants and bushes, they were all sending strands of light to her. Or rather, her body was drawing it out of them. Some smaller than others, indeed some were so small she could hardly see them, but they were there. She headed down through the car park and onto the road, the world looked the same except it was empty. Not a single person, car, or even animal could be seen or heard. Despite this Ellie felt comforted that everything seemed normal, at least until she started walking down the hill. This side of the hill had views of the canal and the surrounding areas, as she was walking, she noticed a dark set of clouds that appeared to be gathering on the horizon. As she watched she realised they were much closer than that and were not in keeping with the rest of the weather she could see. Pausing she looked around, everywhere was clear blue sky with small white clouds. Then there was this one patch of now black clouds getting bigger and bigger. They appeared to be forming above the canal, not far from where Ellie had often met her friends. She stared for a minute or two, watching the clouds get darker and darker, then with a blinding flash there was a huge bolt of light that slammed into the ground. The impact caused the Earth to shake beneath Ellie's feet. Looking in the direction of the clouds, she could see they had started to turn in a circle creating a whirlpool of black clouds around bolts of light that hit the ground repeatedly over and over. Each sending shockwaves through the ground to Ellie's feet. Then to Ellie's horror she realised that one of the bolts of light was heading straight for her. Frozen with fear all she could do was stare at it as it got closer, as if time had been slowed down. Then moments before it struck her, she fell with a thump to the floor of Annabelle's living room. Sitting up immediately, covered in a cold sweat and breathing heavily, Ellie put her head in her hands to try and make sense of what she had just seen.

After sitting for a while, Ellie decided she needed a shower and hoped that Annabelle would not mind. It helped. The warm water flowing over her helped her wash away the confusion and feelings after her dream. She had decided that's what it was, a dream. She examined her palms, other than the mark from the rock there were no markings from the light that she had seen. Indeed, she could feel nothing from the beams of light entering her body. After drying herself, she got dressed again. She had taken her clothes into the bathroom in case Annabelle came home, she did not want to be caught in a towel by her, Emilia, or anyone really. Looking in the mirror she did her best with her hair and made sure she looked presentable. She heard the front door open.
"Ellie, I'm back," Annabelle called.
"Coming," Ellie shouted back. She took a deep breath and left the bathroom. Halfway down the stairs she stopped, stunned. She was greeted not just by Annabelle but by her friends Leo, Dan, and most importantly, Simon.
For a few moments nobody spoke, Ellie stared at the four faces looking back at her and they all stared back kindly.

"She's not an animal in a zoo you know," Annabelle eventually said, breaking the silence. "Let's all go and get a drink and then we can talk."

They all moved into the kitchen, Annabelle hanging back to meet Ellie at the bottom of the stairs.

"Sorry, the day went a bit sideways, Emilia lost it and they, well, they are intrigued but I think they really want to help," she smiled kindly.

"That's ok, I can't thank you enough," Ellie said truthfully. She wanted more time to deal with her dream and what that meant, but she was also appreciative that Annabelle had been able to get them all together so quickly. She smiled and followed Annabelle into the kitchen.

"So, this is weird," Simon said, smiling at Ellie. "You know us, but we don't know you? That about the size of it?"

Ellie grinned, "Yeup, and the good news is you haven't changed at all."

They all chuckled, and Ellie felt the small amount of tension in the room lift almost immediately. Annabelle made drinks for everyone, and as she did so Ellie exchanged pleasantries with the boys. It was a strange situation, Ellie knew them and was acting as if she had always been there, and as the conversations went on they began to warm to her as well, accepting that she was someone they could trust and listen to. Ellie felt at home within minutes of talking to them all and was starting to settle right in with her friends as if nothing had ever happened or changed. After a little while they were all sat around the kitchen table, Annabelle by Ellie's side with Simon to Ellie's right at the end of the table. Leo and Dan were sat opposite. They all turned to Ellie.

"So," Simon began, "we are here to listen, given what we have already heard we know you know us, and we don't know what is going on, but it is weird. So, can you tell us your side of the story?" he smiled kindly.

Ellie took a deep breath, "Ok, I'll tell you everything, then can we link that with what Emilia has said and go from there? See if they match up at all?"

Nobody suggested otherwise, so Ellie began.

"First, thank you for agreeing to listen. I know how crazy this sounds but it means a lot that you are even here. So, do you want me to go right back to the beginning when I first faced off against the Man? Or just skip to the last few days?"

"The beginning," Simon answered on behalf of the group, "We want to see what lines up and matches."

Ellie smiled, "Ok, here goes."

Ellie told her story, she explained how she had faced off against the Man, that Annabelle had kissed her for the first time on the hill that night. The group agreed that all matched what had happened with Emilia. When Ellie covered the arguments, they also agreed these were the same but appeared to be less confrontational. Ellie's version of events seemed to be more reasonable but otherwise the same. Even down to the walking up to the folly and the buzzing by the rocks matched. Where the story started to change was after that. They were astounded at what Ellie told them, the way the man trapped her, tormented her, sent her back in time and apparently gloated over her was unlike anything they had heard before. Ellie continued with their words of encouragement and support helping her along. They noted that her recollection of meeting Emilia on the hill was the same, except Ellie's view was that it was an accident and she did not know what was going on at the time. Emilia's had made out that Ellie had almost attacked her. Ellie kept going until she reached this morning, when Annabelle had left her.

"And then Annabelle left and now here you all are," she said in conclusion.

She decided to pause and take stock before going into the dream that she had and confusing them even more.

"Wow," Simon said. "That is, incredible."

"Everything matches, the only bits that we didn't know or are different are the being trapped, that didn't happen to Emilia," Leo stated.

"Nor the going back in time stuff," Dan added.

"Then the rest is points of view, she sees almost everything as a confrontation," Simon concluded.

Ellie noticed Annabelle was quiet and looking a little glum, she decided to act, "Can we not make this about comparing Emilia and I? She is still the same person as am I, but I don't want to upset anyone."

She squeezed Annabelle's hand under the table and to her surprise, Annabelle squeezed hers back.

"Sorry, you're right," Simon agreed. "I didn't mean anything by it Annabelle."

Annabelle smiled and seemed to relax again; Ellie did not want her to feel guilty for helping her.

"What now then?" Annabelle asked as nobody was saying anything.

"I think we need to write this down and make a plan," Leo answered positively.

There were words of agreement and with that they set about doing so. Ellie and Annabelle collected the one they started the night before while the boys cleared the table. Ellie laid out the timeline on the table and they all poured over it.

"So, this is what he showed me," Ellie explained. "He went through and showed me these key points and then made a change here." She pointed at the dot on the page.

"So, what change do we think he made?" Simon asked.

"No idea – but clearly something that created a new timeline, removing me from it and creating Emilia instead," Ellie commented.

"Why though? What could he do with that?"

They all looked at each other.

"Why don't we start by looking at the differences in the story, and you and Emilia?" Dan added confidently.

This seemed like a sensible idea, so they got a fresh piece of paper and started to list the key differences between Ellie and Emilia. Doing so took some time, they were there for a couple of hours going through Ellie's story step by step to try and find the differences between the two girls. Eventually they had made a list that had been scribbled in Annabelle's handwriting.

> 1. *Emilia was not caught by the Man this time, nor was she shown any of the things Ellie had seen in the past*
> 2. *Ellie could remember everything about us all*

> *– but we do not remember her. Although we all agree that there is something about her that we recognise*
> 3. *Emilia generally reacted to this with anger, Ellie with curiosity*
> 4. *They both don't like the attention they get, but Emilia really hates it and wants it to stop*

"Is that it?" Ellie asked.

"I think so," Annabelle replied, "Your stories and events seem almost identical, even down to the time and reason you moved to the village."

"So, what is the Man up to then? What is he trying to do?"

Nobody knew the answer to this, it was a question that they all needed to understand but could not. Ellie felt that the answer was close, as if it was right there but she could not quite see it.

"Annabelle, can we get some food? And whilst we eat, there is something else that I think I need to share with you all," Ellie added.

They all looked at her.

"Let me explain," she added quickly. "Everything there is true and in the right order, there is nothing missing from that. But there is something else that happened after you left this morning that I haven't told anyone. I'm sorry, but it freaked me out and I was trying to work out how to tell you all on top of all this without it being even more of a crazy thing."

To Ellie's surprise, they all just smiled at her, then Leo spoke.

"We get it Ellie. This is crazy and whilst it is strange and difficult for us, it must be so tough on you. It's fine. Also, I agree, food please," he grinned.

Ellie found it strange that they were warming to her so quickly, she was not complaining but it was odd. Even down to them calling her Ellie, it is what she wanted them to call her but it felt alien for some reason. She could not quite place why.

They ordered Chinese, and later that evening they were all

tucking in to various dishes. The distraction was welcome, for a couple of hours they did not look at the lists they had made or discuss them. Ellie was waiting to tell them about the dream, and they were waiting to hear it. After they had all stopped eating, Ellie decided now was the time to share the last piece of her story.

"Ok, this happened after Annabelle left to meet you all this morning. I was watching TV and drifted off to sleep, nothing strange about that."

"Agree, can we add 'falls asleep easily as she is lazy' to the list of things that are the same as Emilia please?" Simon offered up.

There was a moments laughter, then Ellie continued.

"Thanks for that. I am not lazy. Anyway, I fell asleep and had what I think was a dream. It was like the ones where the Man had come to me before, except it was just me and I was in control. I woke up in my house, in my room. And it was mine, all the photos were of me and stuff. I noticed that the stone key in the garden was glowing and sending the beam of light up towards the folly. You all know about the energy flow up there yes?" she wanted to make sure they knew what she was talking about before going too far.

They nodded in agreement.

"Yeah, Emilia had told us about that," Dan confirmed.

Nodding herself, Ellie continued, "Ok, well, this is where it gets really odd. I noticed that there were beams of light moving to the stone from everything in the garden that was living. Plants, trees, grass, all of it. They were all sending energy to the stone, it was then sending it up to the folly."

"Like the five keys and the lock stuff you mean?" Leo asked.

"Yes, exactly like that. The energy flow from all living things in our world to Imaginari. The stuff that he told me about years ago, the energy that he wants to steal to make his world a physical one."

"Ok, keep going," Annabelle added.

They were all leaning in now, hanging on Ellie's every word.

"Ok, I went over to the tree and noticed that I could draw the energy into me, through my hand," she paused.

"What?" Simon asked.

"It looked as if I was able to draw out the energy as well, as soon as I got close to anything living, the beams of light reached into me. They made my hand glow and tingle. Anyway, I went back into the house and out the front door. It was glowing, and I was curious. When I opened it, I appeared on top of the hill by the folly." She stopped for a drink and a mouthful of rice. Nobody spoke, they just waited until she carried on. "Up there was the same thing, I could see the five beams from the keys going to the folly. And anything living would send strands of light into my hands, legs, arms, everywhere. Sending a tingle all over and leaving no marks or anything. There wasn't anything else to see or do so I started walking down the hill, in my head heading home. Then as I could see out over the views, a huge black cloud appeared sending a bolt of light into the ground that made it shake over and over. Finally, a single bolt of light headed for me and that's when I woke up. I fell on the floor covered in a cold sweat and really confused. That's it," she finished, sat back and looked around waiting for the responses and questions.

Annabelle spoke first, "So, you're saying in the dream you could draw energy from anything living in the same way the stone keys do?"

"Seemed like it."

"And nothing like that has happened before? Never been another dream or something that has made you think this was possible?"

"Nope, never. First time, and the Man never mentioned anything like that. It was as if I could work within that energy flow for some reason. It was really odd."

"Have you tried to do it since the dream? For real I mean," Simon asked, curiosity showing all over his face.

"Tried what?"

"Moving near something living to see what happens," he confirmed.

"Oh, no," the thought had not occurred to Ellie. She stood and headed over to a potted plant in the corner of the room. Ellie could feel four sets of eyes following her silently as she did so. She held her palm by the leaves of the plant and bent in close to look, she concentrated hard. Nothing. "Nothing," she said, without turning and keeping her hand near the plant.

This was greeted by four sighs from behind her.

"Maybe try something outside?" Dan suggested.

Ellie turned and headed out of the back door. It was a quiet evening; the sun was setting, and the evening chill had started to settle. She walked out onto the grass and towards a large bush at the far end of the garden. The others followed but stayed a distance back, nerves clearly showing. Ellie approached the bush and put her palm out towards it. She focused hard, trying to remember what it felt like in her dream to have these beams of light moving into her hand. Closing her eyes, she thought harder than she had ever thought about anything before.

"Anything?" Annabelle asked from back by the house.

For anyone watching this would have looked odd, five friends in a garden, one standing by a bush holding their hands out with their eyes closed, and the other four watching on from a distance as though at a fireworks display.

Ellie was about to respond when she felt the slightest tingle in the tip of the fingers on her right hand. She opened her eyes to look. So faint it was almost invisible, was a small strand of golden light flowing from the bush into her palm.

"It's doing it," she shouted.

Immediately the others moved quickly across the grass to see.

"There is nothing there," Simon commented, peering round at her hands.

"Yeah, nothing," Leo agreed.

"I can feel it and see it," Ellie defended. "It's only faint but it is there."

She was feeling the pressure of expectation, she needed them to see and believe her.

"Ellie, is it possible you want to believe this so much that you are imagining it?" Dan commented bravely.

"I'm not making it up," Ellie pleaded. "Ok, everyone back away again and let me focus on this."

They did as she asked and fell silent. She closed her eyes once more and focused her mind.

"Ellie," Annabelle called.

"Shhhh," She replied.

"Eleanor," Simon and Annabelle said in unison.

"What?" she snapped, turning around. "I'm trying to prove to you that-"

She cut herself off, distracted by the four friends who were no longer looking at her, but were looking at the sky above. She turned to look at what they were looking at, over the hill the sky had turned black, covered in clouds that were twisting and turning like the sea in a storm.

Ellie backed up until she was in a line with the others, "Well, that matches my dream at least."

They all looked up, mesmerized by the storm that had appeared out of nowhere.

"No lightning though," Simon commented, more out of hope than anything else. "Let's go inside and think about this."

Without another word, they all turned and ran quickly inside.

"Ok, whatever he is doing it is happening now, what did we miss? What am I missing by being the odd one out here?" Ellie implored them all, looking over the notes they had made.

"What if, we have this backwards?" Simon asked, he had stopped short of the table.

They all looked at him.

"Hear me out. We have assumed that the change he made took Ellie out of the timeline, and put Emilia in, yeah? What if that's wrong? What if the change he made simply added Emilia to the timeline and in doing so made us all forget Ellie? Putting Emilia in her place."

"But why? What would that do?" Dan asked.

They were all thinking it.

"It must be something that is happening now. He said to you Ellie that he didn't want to change anything that had already happened, yeah?"

Ellie nodded, going along with Simon's thought process for now.

"Right, so he didn't want to change any of that which is why the stories match up until now. He wants Emilia to act differently than Ellie would to something that is happening now."

Ellie's eyes lit up, that made sense, "I think you're onto something there, keep going," she said encouragingly.

He moved back to the window, looking out at the storm he carried on, "Ellie, would you say that you fell asleep early afternoon?"

"I guess."

"And that you woke up somewhere between three and four?"

"Yes, why? What's that got to do with it?"

"And you woke up at the moment you saw the storm being formed in your dream, the same as that one there?" There was a stern tone to his voice now.

"Simon, she has told us this," Annabelle pleaded.

"It's ok, yes, that's right," Ellie added.

Simon turned to face them. "Ellie, in your dream were you facing over the view where the Brown Dog pub where we were sat at would have been?"

She nodded, "I think so, yes."

His eyes widened with fear, "In that case, that means that Ellie saw the storm clouds build and the bolt of lightning hit at around the time that Emilia was losing it and shouting at us. More to the point she saw it happen over where we actually were, right before she stormed off back up the hill."

He turned back to the window, looking up at the clouds, "I think, he added Emilia so that she would act angrily and lash out at the positive attention she has been getting after beating him the first time. Think about it, she hates it and would do anything to be rid of it."

Ellie moved to be by his side, looking up at the sky.

He continued, "I think Emilia is more him than you right now, I think he is using her anger to get his way. That's why he didn't want to change anything that had happened, he needed that to make her angry and resent the victory."

In Ellie's mind, it all slotted into place, "So, you think that he is using her anger to break down the barrier? To get what he wants?"

He nodded silently, the others moved close to them, so they were now all looking out of the window at the storm over the hill.

"And the bolt of light I saw in my dream?" she asked nervously.

"Was the moment that he took over her mind and filled it with rage," Simon finished for her, "then she went storming off back to the place he knows best."

"The top of Mow Cop," Ellie added.

The five friends looked at the black clouds building and swirling, it did all make sense and was the only thing that at least covered everything they knew. As they looked, a huge bolt of light tore across the sky. Lighting up the hill as it did so for a moment revealing the folly as a silhouette against the sky.

"Then that is where I need to go," Ellie stated solemnly.

CHAPTER 10

Emilia.

Emilia slowly stood, still clutching her arm to try and keep it still. The pain was there mostly when her arm moved so she was doing her best to keep it still. She closed her eyes and took a deep breath, then slowly turned around. She opened her eyes. Right in front of her, floating a few feet above the ground, was the Man Of Mow. Emilia knew that if he could smile, he would be.

"Been looking for you," she stated coldly.

"Indeed, so I have heard," he replied in his usual annoyingly calm voice. "But I wonder if you understand why you have been looking for me?"

Emilia's eyes narrowed, "What is there to understand?"

He chuckled, "There is more at play here than you will ever know. And unlike before, I am prepared for everything you can do or think of, because I am going to be victorious."

"Ok, pretty sure that I don't know what you mean. What makes you think you will beat me this time? Actually, what are you doing here? I thought I beat you for good?"

"Of course, you do not have the complete picture, you can only recall on the memories that are relevant. You don't know the full story; would you like me to reveal the truth to you?"

Emilia let go of her arm, "You have lied to me before," she challenged, "Why should I believe you now?"

He floated in her direction, putting himself directly in front of her. "Because you are going to help me win. You, Emilia, are the missing piece of the puzzle. There is nothing you can do to change that, so I will share it with you."

He raised his arms out sideways, then brought them together quickly in front of him with a loud clapping bang.

The moment his hands met; the hill disappeared around Emilia. She was left standing surrounded by purple smoke. Emilia knew this place; she knew now that he was sharing a vision with her.

"What now then?" she asked.

"I want to tell you the truth about the energy that I crave so much from your world. What it can really do."

"You told me before, you want to use all of it at once to make Imaginari a physical world. We have been through this already."

"Yes, we have, but I want to show you what it can really do."

The landscape changed around Emilia's feet, she was now standing on top of the hill by the folly, but it was not real. It looked like a shadow representation of the hill as if drawn in nothing but charcoal, though tinted with purple. The smoke like vapour was forming the shapes of the hill, rocks, and the folly but it was always moving and flowing around.

"This is how my world would create the hill that you know so well. See how it exists but if you touch any of it, it immediately dissolves and then reforms after you have moved away."

Emilia tried this, she reached out to touch a tree and as she did, her hand moved through the vapour dissolving that part of the tree. Once her hand had gone it reformed in front of her eyes.

"So?" she asked. "You're made of the same stuff, aren't you? Why does it matter when you're not able to touch anything anyway?" This was cold from Emilia and she knew it, but she also knew she needed to stay strong and keep pushing him.

"Yes, we are made of the same, stuff, as you put it. But I can interact with it, watch."

He moved over to the same tree and picked a leaf from it, he held it out to her in his bony hand.

Emilia tried to take it, but it dissolved as soon as she touched it in the same way the tree had.

"I'm confused," Emilia commented. "It looks like your world is already solid enough?"

"No, not at all," he picked another leaf. "Watch."

He held it in front of her, but this time Emilia watched rather than reaching out for it. As she watched, the leaf first began to shimmer then after a few seconds with a small pop it exploded into smoke.

Emilia jumped back, "What happened? Why did it do that?"

"The energy can only sustain the contact for a short time, then it dissolves in a permanent way, this leaf and its energy is now gone for good. Therefore, we need more of the energy from your world. I believe that if we pull it all through in one go, we can force it into everything and then our world will begin to take form and we can start to live the way we want to."

Emilia backed away, "That sounds like you're not even sure it will work?"

He faced her, "Indeed there is a chance that it would not, but I believe that it will. And I have come too far to not complete my mission."

"And what would happen to our world after this?" Emilia asked, concern creeping into her voice now.

"Your world would be reduced to host only non-living things, stone, metal, and ash. Then we will come forth to your land and put our energy over this landscape of yours; creating a brilliant world that is physical and eternal."

His tone became confident now, clearly enjoying revealing all of this to Emilia.

"So, you would kill everything in our world, to then move from yours into ours? That it?"

"Well done child, you understand. I admit this was not my original thought, as at first, I simply wanted to make my world real and stay there. I have since realised that moving to yours is a much stronger idea and will allow us to create something special."

"And you think I will help you with this?" Emilia asked defiantly.

"Were you not just saying how you wanted to get your life back? How you would do anything to make all this stop?"

"Yes, but it sounds like I will be killed too. That hardly gives me my life back does it?"

Emilia folded her arms, she was beginning to regret her words that she has said in anger on the hill.

"I can offer you an alternative, I can give you back your life exactly as it was."

"How?" she was not sure what to believe or think, but she knew she needed to keep him talking.

He moved towards her, "Like this."

He then moved through her, and as he did so Emilia felt a cold chill spread over her body. She turned to face him. He was facing her once more but next to her was a floating spirit. It looked familiar; it took a few seconds for Emilia to realise who it was. It was her; she was looking at a spirit version of herself.

"This is you, or rather, the spirit you. It has your consciousness, your memories, but most of all it is like me and so can live in our spirit world."

Emilia stared at it, at herself. She found it very unnerving, "So, you want to turn me into one of these things?" she asked.

"My child, you already are one of these things, these spirits exist in every living thing, all I want to do is set yours free and allow it to live in Imaginari. And then, your world."

He clapped his hands together once more, and the hill was immediately replaced by a large flat piece of land. As Emilia watched it took shape and form, there was a metal fence around the edge. There were benches along paths, bushes and trees appeared too.

"I know this place," Emilia whispered, "This is the park in London where I used to hang out with Sophie and the girls."

"Yes, it can be yours once again."

"But I can't enjoy any of it can I?" she walked over to a bench and tried to sit on it, "See, it just vanishes."

He said nothing, then reached out to point at Emilia. He appeared to grab an invisible rope and pulled.

Emilia felt like she was going to sleep but then immediately woke up again. She had moved, she was no longer near the bench facing the Man. She was now next to him, looking at her own body frozen in front of her. "What have you done?"

she shouted, looking down at her hands. Her ghost like hands made of mist and vapour.

The Man turned to face her, "I have moved your consciousness to your spirit form, you are now like me. Try the bench this time."

Without thinking Emilia floated over to the bench past her own body. It was still upright but her eyes were closed, and she looked to be in a deep sleep. She turned and sat on the bench, it supported her.

"See, if you help me, and allow me to give you this, you can have it all back."

He raised his arms once more and suddenly the park was filled with recreations of people.

A group behind the Man caught Emilia's eye. She stood and moved over to them. It was her old friends, Sophie, Tina, and Lara. She floated near them as they did not seem to notice her. They were too busy chatting and giggling to themselves.

"You can go back home, your real home. You can leave all the pain behind you and live forever in a glorious eternal world," he sounded triumphant as if this would convince Emilia to help him. "You can have whatever you want, Emilia. But only if you help me."

He made the same pulling gesture once more and Emilia had the same sleep and wake feeling. She was now back in her own body; the spirit form had also vanished and it was just her and the Man once again.

Emilia was stunned and confused, there was a feeling deep in her gut though, a feeling so strong that she was finding it hard to ignore. A feeling that she desperately wanted to get her old life back, a life before Mow Cop. She looked up at the Man.

"You know it is true, you know you want this, all you have to do is willingly say yes and I will make it so."

"You're saying if I help you, I will get my old life back? No more thanks, no more link to you, just me and my old friends?"

He said nothing, but just looked at her plainly.

"All the pain and anger will stop?"

Still nothing.

"What makes you think I am so selfish? I'd lose Annabelle and the others as well."

The silence was deafening for Emilia now.

Then it came to her, like a distant memory or thought from long ago that she had forgotten all about. She wanted this, she wanted to go back home. Emilia had never been happy, not really since she left London. He was offering her a way out, not an ideal way but a way none the less. Emilia felt as though she was losing control, but she could not stop it. To Emilia's shock and without really thinking about it the words fell out of her mouth.

"Ok, I will help you."

Then it went dark, as if she was falling asleep.

Emilia stirred, she tried to move her arms but could not. She lifted her head and looked around, she was back in the realm of purple smoke and vapour. She tried to move but could not. Then she noticed the reason for this was that she was bound at the wrists, she was standing but her arms and legs were being held fast with golden strands of light pulling her into a star shape. In front of her the Man was facing away muttering to himself, Emilia closed her eyes to try and clear her head and focus on what he was saying.

"So close, she has agreed and now I have the power I need in my grasp. You, you will be the difference my child, you are now everything I need," he turned to face Emilia and moved to be right in front of her face. "You will not die quickly, Emilia, you will watch as your world burns."

Emilia opened her eyes, she did not really mean to, but it just happened.

"Ahhhhh so you are awake," he gloated, backing away a little.

"What do you want from me?" she pleaded, struggling against her bonds.

He chuckled, "My child, you have already given it to me," he moved to the side revealing the floating spirit Emilia once more. "By agreeing to give me your soul I have been able to remove your spirit energy, permanently. And the best part, it is now mine to control, all I need to do is take it to the stones and the energy will be so great that the barrier will be torn down. Then all the energy from your world will flow into mine."

Emilia froze, the realisation of his words hitting her like a train, "You were never going to let me live, were you?"

"Oh yes I am, or at least your spirit will. You will fade I'm afraid, slowly you will perish but not before you have seen the sky torn apart by the portal failing."

"Why did you need me for that? Why my spirit?"

"Because I made you. I made this version of you to be so angry and resentful that it would store up all the energy it could but do it in a way that would build and build until eventually you would give in to me. In doing so, your spirit would come to me and aid me."

"You, made me?" Emilia was confused, "What do you mean?"

He laughed a loud booming laugh, "Yes, I made you. See if you can figure it out. But for now, I think I can release you back to your world."

Almost instantly, the purple smoke vanished and the bonds holding Emilia up were released. She dropped to her knees onto the cold grass. They were back on top of the hill by the folly, as far as Emilia could tell it was real and was not long after she had arrived at the rocks. She was alone with the Man and the spirit that was clearly her. It had no colour other than a faint yellow, it had her features, but they were lifeless. To Emilia it looked like a waxwork of herself, floating above the ground following the Man wherever he went.

"So, here we are, your world, your time. Just in time in fact for me to carry out my plan," he gloated.

"I won't let you get away with this," Emilia said through gritted teeth as she stood, almost immediately her right leg gave way. She looked down confused by it as she fell to the floor.

"You are already weakening. Did I forget to mention that you cannot survive without your spirit here? Although, yours was so filled with anger and hate that it would not have been much use anyway."

Emilia looked at him and forced herself to get up.

"I will stop this," she was trying to be brave and sound strong, but her voice was weakening.

The Man moved over to her, "It is too late. I have already won. There is nothing that you, or Eleanor, or anyone can do."

Emilia focused, latching onto one key word that he had just said. "Eleanor?" Emilia thought hard, she was trying to make sense of it all, was she connected to Eleanor from the hill somehow?

He lifted himself away from her, "It is too late now, all you can do is watch as I carry out the final steps to my plan."

He moved away from Emilia and the folly, down the crest of the hill with Emilia's spirit following behind like a dog following its owner.

Emilia started to follow too, it took a huge amount of effort to move, she felt as though she had a bad cold or flu, as if all the energy had been removed from her in one go. She knew she could not give up though, she had to try and get help. Annabelle, Simon, Leo, anyone to help her stop him and his plan. All she could think though was that it was too little too late, she had been so filled with anger and revenge that she had fallen straight into his trap and given him exactly what he wanted. Emilia felt deflated and defeated, but she knew she had to try.

After what felt like an age she eventually rounded the corner and could see the Statue Of Mow. To her horror it appeared she was already too late. The Man was floating above the rocks, arms outstretched. At her level was her spirit, floating in the same way slowly turning around. Emilia struggled to get closer, it was getting tough now, she was almost having to support her body on all fours to keep moving. Eventually she made it to the fence that surrounded the Statue Of Mow, she supported herself on it and surveyed the scene. Despite everything, Emilia found it devastating to think that she was looking at her own spirit do something so evil, she did not know what to do.

"You are too late," the Man called down. "It has already begun."

Emilia looked up; the sky had turned black filled with swirling clouds. The only sources of light were now the Man himself, and Emilia's spirit, everything else appeared to be covered in what looked like a black sheet that sucked the light out of every surface. Emilia lifted herself over the barrier.

"It is never too late," she called weakly.

She sounded braver than she felt. She started to move towards her spirit, reaching out for it. Emilia felt that if she could get it back it would help her think clearly.

"It will not work, girl," he shouted down at her. "In moments we will have entered my world and your spirit will be gone for good. Even if you could get it back, it would resist you now after you released it to me."

Emilia ignored him and kept pushing forward, reaching out a hand. She did not know why but she thought that if she could just touch it something would happen. Closer and closer she edged, she started to get the same feeling as when approaching these very rocks earlier that day. A buzzing feeling running through her arm and up into her body. It started to resist and push her back, but Emilia used every ounce of strength she had left to push on. At the final moment, her hand touched the hand of her spirit and at that very moment, a bolt of light tore across the sky. It went through the Man, into the Statue Of Mow then out into Emilia's spirit. As it hit her spirit the force blasted Emilia back. She was blown through the fence and ended up in a heap on the ground. She lifted her head up, she saw the Man and her spirit vanish into thin air moments after she was able to focus on them. Leaving behind a shaking hilltop covered by dark clouds. She tried to sit up but could not. She lay back down, and her eyes forced themselves to close. The last thoughts to pass through her mind was that she needed to get help, then there was nothing.

CHAPTER 11

Ellie.

The five friends stood and watched, all waiting for another bolt of light or something to happen. Nothing did. Eventually Annabelle broke the silence.

"You can't just go up there and say, 'hey guys what's happening' can you?"

Ellie looked at her, "What do you suggest?"

Annabelle said nothing.

"I have to try, and if we are right that Emilia is somehow being manipulated, or was created by him, I may be the only one that can get through to her and stop all this," she turned to get ready.

"Ok, at least let us go with you," Annabelle implored.

Ellie turned to face them all again, "I can't ask you to do that, I can't ask you to come and deal with whatever is going on up there."

"You let us help you before," Simon commented sheepishly.

Ellie was taken aback by this, "You mean Emilia, you helped Emilia not me."

"We don't know that, for all we know you are one and the same. We have never seen you in the same place," Dan added, with the sort of tone that suggested he wanted to join in as best as he could.

"That's a good point," Leo agreed.

Ellie rubbed her face in frustration, covering her eyes, "Fine. But we need a plan, we can't just go running up there waving our arms around can we." Ellie stormed away to get some peace, heading into the toilet, and splashing some cold water on her face. Looking in the mirror, water dripping down her chin into the basin, "What do we do?" she asked her reflection. "What have we got on our side? Last time we had the stones and staffs on our side, but that was used by the folly, I don't think that will work for the statue." She turned off the tap, dried her face and stood tall in front of the mirror. Exhaling she challenged herself, "Come on Ellie, you can do this," with that she left the room and went back to the others. Walking back into the kitchen she was greeted by faces of sympathy and support. "Sorry, I didn't mean to snap. This is not how I saw my day going is all and you have all done so much already."

They all smiled at her; Anabelle spoke first, "Hardly. All we have done is talk and listen for a couple of hours."

"I didn't mean just tonight," tears starting to show in Ellie's eyes now. "I can't keep asking you to help me."

"Technically," Simon interrupted. "You haven't asked us to do anything, that was Emilia as you said. Besides, we want to help because we kind of have a connection to the world we live in and stuff," he smirked.

Ellie was speechless, she knew these people were her friends, but she had still not got used to them being so supportive, especially as technically they did not know her right now.

"So, what do we do then?" she asked.

"I think the key is you," Leo commented.

"Well yes, the Man has chosen her from centuries ago, if it's the same as Emilia that is," Annabelle stated.

"Yes, but what I mean is the energy flow thing," Leo explained. "Emilia never had that, and I'm guessing you didn't either?"

Ellie shook her head, "No not until now."

"Right, what if that is a side effect of whatever he did to you, whatever he did to make Emilia may have given you an advantage he didn't know about."

That made sense. This was new, and she had not heard anything about it before.

"You think he gave me a way to interact with the energy flow? Why? How?"

"Maybe he didn't mean it," Leo added. "Maybe when he did whatever he did to your spirit it opened up what was left to allow you to see and interact with it. We know that it flows from our world into his, yes? That is why he wants to rip down the barriers between worlds, to take it all at once."

Ellie nodded, "That is, or at least was, his plan yes. He wants to use the energy from all living things here to make his world a physical one by taking it all at once."

"So, maybe now you can use that?"

"I have no idea how to use it, it took me ages to get the tiniest little bit of it, not sure that will be much help."

"Ok, I have an idea," Simon jumped in. "We can work together; you will need us to convince Emilia. If we are right, then she will be up there right now doing something crazy and won't listen to you because she thinks you're the one the Man wants. So, here is what we do. We all go to the hill, Ellie you try and figure out as fast as you can if you can use this energy, the rest of us will get there and try to talk Emilia round to working with you," he said this with such confidence that Ellie was a little speechless.

"Ok, I think I know where to go and try, Annabelle can I borrow your bike?"

Annabelle nodded, "Go, we will set off for the hill."

Ellie paused for a moment, "I'm going to go home. That is where I was in the dream when the energy was strong. There and the folly but I can't go there. Going to see what I can do; I'll meet you by the Statue Of Mow as soon as I can."

Then she turned and left the room.

Shortly after, Ellie was pedalling fast on Annabelle's bike. She had a plan but knew she had limited time to do anything. After about fifteen minutes of cycling at a reasonable pace Ellie slowed down, she was exhausted and was nearly home but needed to be careful. She got off the bike and hid it inside a bush, then she crept along the road towards the top of her driveway. Or as she noted to herself several times, Emilia's driveway. To Ellie's relief there were no lights on, "Nicholas and Katherine must be in bed," she said to herself quietly as she crept down the driveway, she could not bring herself to call them mum and dad right now. Ellie climbed over the side gate and went down the path to the garden. She checked the kitchen windows and still nothing, breathing a little calmer she headed over to the stone and sat down by it. Ellie knew that this would only work for living things, but she felt that the connection to the stone would help her somehow. The grass was cold but not damp as she rested her palms on the ground and closed her eyes. She exhaled and focused her mind reminding herself of what it felt like to feel the energy flowing into her palms. She needed to focus on the tingling and buzzing feeling that spread through her body. Everything went quiet, Ellie could no longer hear the wind in the trees or distant cars driving by. It was just her, the ground, and her mind. She opened her eyes; the garden had gone. Or rather, the stone, trees, bushes, and hedges had gone. Only the grass remained for as far as she could see. Ellie forced herself to remain calm, this was not real, but it felt different to every other moment she had experienced like this and she needed to see it through.

"Hello?" she asked nervously.

There was a sound like a sliding door opening that echoed all around her. She looked from left to right, nothing. Then the sound came again, Ellie focused on it and realised it sounded like heavy breathing. Soft but not comforting, the sound she imagined a dragon or large fictional animal would sound like.

"Hello," she said again, firmer this time.

"We hear you," came a voice that sounded like it was being spoken by someone with a chest infection. It sounded like someone that needed help breathing or was having to work hard to do so. "We are here because you need our help. We need to help you to allow you to save both worlds."

Ellie paused to work this out, then shook her head to clear it, "What? Simple please! Are you here to help me, or help him, the Man?"

There was another deep breath, "We are the same as him when it comes to where we are from and what we are made of. But he is very different when it comes to what he wants."

"So, you want to stop him?" Ellie tried to clarify.

"We want both worlds to survive. We are the Guardians of Imaginari."

Ellie concluded that was something and meant that she could probably trust whoever this was, "Guardians? Why have you not come to me before, or better yet stopped him yourself?"

"We are not able to stop him from our world, for he is the strongest of us, he has taken our forms meaning we now can only exist as thoughts."

"So, you can't take form like he can? Is that why I can't see you?"

There was a pause then Ellie was surrounded by a grey mist, as if she was standing on top of a high hill in the clouds.

"We can form only like this, but we can do this in both your world and ours. Where our worlds are close."

"So, have I seen you before? In my world I mean?"

"Yes, your people have seen us like this for centuries. We exist and move across the sky, soaking up the energy that we need and transporting it to our world."

"You're, the clouds?" she asked, wondering if she was understanding correctly.

"That is one of our many forms yes. We exist in harmony with your world, soaking up only what is needed and depositing the balance back to you in liquid form."

"You mean rain? You're telling me that you appear to us as clouds, soaking up the energy you need from our world then putting it into yours? Then what you don't need you put back onto our world as rain?" Ellie was stunned but somehow this fitted and made sense to her.

"Correct. We move to the weak points between our worlds, such as the hill in your village, and move the energy. The one you call the Man however, wants to take it all in one go, ripping your world to ruin and forcing ours through onto yours."

"What do you mean, onto mine?"

"He wants to destroy all life on your world, then move our spirit forms in to yours to make a world that is both physical and spirit driven. He wants to merge them, what he does not realise is that this will destroy both eventually. They need each other, but each needs the other to remain separate."

"Ok, so, how do I stop it? That's why you are here yes, to help me?"

"We want to tell you that he has made a mistake, a mistake that may lead to his failure and your victory over him."

"I'm listening."

"Your friend Leo was correct."

Ellie raised her eyebrows, "Really?"

"Yes. When he removed your spirit and spliced it to create Emilia, he did not fully appreciate what he was doing. In our world doing a splice would always lead to changes that were not intended. He took the bit of you he needed to make Emilia. He took your anger, hate, fear, all the negativity he could find to create her."

"Why? Why did he need to do that?"

"He needed a spirit from your world, full of anger and given willingly. By using this spirit, he can destroy the barrier between our worlds. The power it will unleash will be too strong for it to contain. He will try to pull it into his prison realm, once in there it will grow in strength until it all falls apart around him. When that happens, nothing will stop him."

"Ok, so, what do I have to do? How can I stop him?"

"You must use his error. He has given you the ability to use the spirit energy, you must master this and take the child Emilia with you."

"That may be harder than it sounds," Ellie said worryingly. "She doesn't like me much, and I have no idea how to use this energy."

"We have already shown you how."

"That was you in my dream? You brought me here?"

"Yes, we showed you what to do, all you need to do is focus and think. Think about what you want to do, and the energy will flow, it will be invisible to all but you. Draw it from any living thing to you, then move it to any other living thing. Remember, whatever is taken must be returned, there must always be balance. There can never be energy left over, it must all be used."

The mist started to fade around Ellie, "Wait, what about

Emilia, how can she help?"

"What is taken must be returned," came the voice, fading now as the mist started to vanish.

"How do I do this? What do I need to do?"

"You already know, you have always known," then the mist had gone, along with the voice.

Ellie was now back in the garden once more, everything as it was.

"Is that it?" she asked out loud.

Nothing. She sighed and looked down at her hands. They were still on the ground; in fact they had been pushed down into it quite hard by Ellie. The thing that surprised her the most though was that they were glowing golden yellow. Ellie lifted her hands to look at them, they kept their glow for a few moments then Ellie became aware of the tingling sensation spreading up her arms and into her chest. Looking around, she could see all the energy glowing in everything that was living, the stone was absorbing it and sending a beam of light up towards the folly. It was only faint, but she could see it and was strangely comforted in the knowledge that it was invisible to all but her. She looked around, everything was as it was, and Ellie concluded that she was back in the real world once more. These visions and dreams were so frequent and real now that she had to remind herself what was real and what was not each time. Ellie stood, took one last look up at the house and then went back along the side path, over the gate, and up the driveway. Moments later she was back on the road pedalling hard with a new found focus and drive to win again. This was a much harder ride though as it was all uphill with very little respite for her legs as she pushed and pushed. It was dark now; the sky had turned jet black, and all the stars had vanished. Moving through the pools of light from streetlights Ellie pushed on, even though this was her home and she knew it well she had never felt more alone than she did right now. The isolation gave her chance to think and focus her mind. She kept going over in her mind what the so-called Guardians had told her.

"I'm taking advice from clouds now?" she said out loud between deep breaths and panting. "Guardians, not very good at guarding are they," she mused, "Imaginari has got some explaining to do."

Then she moved onto the energy, and how she could try to use it. She looked around, and as she did so she thought about the energy that was flowing through every living thing around her. She wanted to close her eyes to focus but she could not, so she had to think even harder. As she did so, she became aware that she was beginning to be surrounded by light. A faint yellow glow. As Ellie rode the bike up the hill every living thing was pushing energy towards her like tiny strands of string. String that glowed and did not hold her back, instead they gave Ellie a surge of energy and she pushed on, pedalling faster than she had before. The pickup in speed surprised her, then as she realised she was doing it by drawing in the energy from her surroundings she mastered it and used it to push on. She could do this; the confidence began to flow easily and with it the ability to absorb the energy for use she began to understand. She could see each time she exhaled that there were small fragments of light in her breath.

"Always a balance," she said, realising that now. "Anything I use has to go back and anything I don't use will also be given back." This new found understanding gave Ellie another push, another reason to carry on. "Next stop, Emilia," Ellie knew that convincing her to help would be an even bigger challenge. She was hoping against hope that the others had found her and been able to talk some sense into her.

Ellie did not relent, she kept pushing and using as much energy as she could and after a short while she rounded the final corner so that the Statue Of Mow came into view. Ellie stopped to look at the sky, the dark swirling clouds seemed to have got darker and more vicious somehow now that she was up close. To Ellie it was much more intimidating than her first encounter with the Man by the folly a couple of years ago.

"Ellie, quick," Dan's voice broke her out of her momentary trance and she hurried over to where he was beckoning her from, jumping off the bike and letting it fall to the ground.

"What's going on?" she asked, catching her breath as quickly as she could.

"It's Emilia, she's well, come look," he turned and led Ellie away from the statue towards the others.

Ellie being so preoccupied with the sky had not noticed them all huddled in a circle a short distance away. When they got close the others parted and allowed Ellie to see. Her heart sank, lying still on the ground showing no signs of life was Emilia. Ellie hurried over to her side, "Emilia," she called.

"It's no use," Annabelle added with a solemn tone. "We have called an ambulance; they are on their way. She is breathing but won't wake up."

Ellie looked round, Simon was on the phone presumably with the emergency services, he had a very worried look on his face.

"I need her, I can't do this without her," Ellie exclaimed, real fear and panic in her voice now. They all looked at her, confusion on their faces. "It's a long story but, I need her to help me. It's the only way."

"Well, she can't do that now can she," Leo replied.

"How long until the ambulance gets here?" Ellie asked, looking at Simon.

"Five minutes, maybe a little less."

"Ok, everyone back away I need to try something."

Nobody moved, they just looked at Ellie confused.

"Look, I can't do this without her help, if what I am thinking doesn't work then the ambulance will still get here. But I have to try, because without her right now we all lose."

This seemed to work, they all immediately backed away giving Ellie space near Emilia to do what she needed to do.

Ellie took Emilia's hand in hers, it was cold to the touch, but Ellie tried to forget that and carry on. She put her other hand firmly on the ground and closed her eyes. She needed to focus and think.

Energy from the ground, through me and into Emilia, that's what I need, Ellie thought to herself taking deep breaths as she did so.

Clearing her mind of everything else. She felt the isolation beginning to build once more. The wind faded, and the sounds of the hilltop disappeared, all Ellie could hear, and feel, was her own breathing. How long she stayed like that for, Ellie did not know. She could feel the tingling building in her right hand, the one that was on the floor and the warm pulsing sensation moving through her body down to her left hand. The more she focused, the more aware she was of that feeling, the feeling of energy flowing through her from right to left. She pushed hard, knowing that time was against her. She needed to do this before the ambulance arrived and still in time to go after the Man and whatever he was up to.

"Eleanor?" she heard a soft voice say, a voice that sounded weak and distant.

Ellie opened her eyes, and there looking up at her was Emilia. "It worked," she called to the others, they hurried over looks of astonishment all over their faces.

"How, I mean, how?" Annabelle asked, rushing round to support Emilia's head as she was trying to sit up.

"I think I can use the energy flow that he loves so much to our advantage. I think I can actually use it," Ellie explained.

"What happened? Where am I?" Emilia asked, sitting up now and looking around her at the group, "Why are you all here?"

"What's the last thing you remember?" Annabelle asked.

"I remember walking, or stamping, away from you all. I came up to the folly, then the Statue Of Mow and then-" she stopped, closing her eyes in despair. "Then I saw the Man, he explained that I could get everything back as it was if I just helped him," she lowered her head in shame, "I gave in and let him take what he wanted."

"What did he take from you?" Ellie asked, "What happened Emilia, tell us."

Emilia lifted her head, "He took my spirit, saying he had made it and that it had what he needed to destroy the barrier between worlds."

"Where did he take it?"

Emilia nodded towards the statue, "He has taken it to the prison realm-"

"Once there it will get more powerful and destroy the barrier," Ellie finished for her, they all looked at her. "I've learned a lot in the last hour," she said as if this explained everything. "Look I'll explain after we deal with all this ok?"

"What do you think we need to do Eleanor, I mean, Ellie?" Emilia asked.

Ellie was pleasantly surprised by this, "You want to help me?"

"Yes, it feels like the right thing to do. I don't see how I have a choice or how it will make things worse from here."

There was a silent agreement between them at this.

"I think we need to go after him, can you stand?" Ellie asked.

"She can barely sit up," Annabelle defended.

"I have to," Emilia defied, lifting herself onto her knees.

"The reason you're struggling is without a spirit you will have no energy, I helped by pushing some from the grass into you but that won't last long I don't think."

They all stopped and looked at her again.

"You pushed energy from the ground?" Leo asked.

"No time Leo," Emilia said through gritted teeth as she lifted herself to her feet. "We have to try."

Ellie supported under one arm, Annabelle the other and between them they lifted Emilia to her feet.

"What are you going to do?" Anabelle asked.

"We need to get to the statue," Ellie replied, "Emilia and I need to go after him. I think once we are there, she will get her full strength back."

"And if she doesn't?"

"Then we lose," Ellie confirmed in a stern harsh voice.

The two girls supported Emilia step by step, it was slow progress, but it was progress and Ellie was happy that they were working as a team, at least for now anyway. They reached the fence surrounding the statue, the boys going ahead to move the bits of broken wood and break the pieces off the edge to make a big enough gap for the girls to walk through. Step by step they got closer to the statue and Ellie could feel the resistance building once more, like an invisible barrier keeping them away from it.

"Keep pushing," she said to Annabelle, "We can get through this just keep going."

They moved closer and closer, with each step the resistance getting stronger. They were within touching distance of the stone now, Ellie reached out her hand, the same hand that she had used earlier before all of this started. She pushed it onto the surface of the rock and with a bang and flash of blinding light she found herself supporting Emilia alone, surrounded by purple smoke and vapour. The hilltop was nowhere to be seen.

CHAPTER 12

Emilia.

Emilia's head was spinning. She was trying to process everything that had happened and what it all meant. Even though she had woken up a few minutes ago, she was still processing what she had seen. The first thing she could recall was the feeling of being drained when he removed her spirit from her body and kept it for himself. She had never felt so weak as when she was trying to follow him over the hilltop. She remembered the Man floating above the statue with her spirit there as well, gloating that it was too late and all she could do was watch as the world was destroyed. The bolt of lightning that blasted her across the hilltop was also fresh in her mind, as were the aches and pains that pulsated all over her body. The strangest memory was the feeling of warmth spreading through her body just before she woke up. Emilia imagined it felt the same as if you ran a bath whilst sat in it, allowing the warmth to gently build around you, eventually submerging you in warm, comforting, liquid. When she woke to find Ellie holding her hand as the apparent source of warmth it threw her, but also convinced her that listening to her was the right thing to do. She knew she was in the wrong the moment that the Man tricked her into releasing her spirit. Now here she was, surrounded by purple smoke and vapour being held up by the girl that she now knew was a part of her. Most of all that they needed to work together to stand any chance of beating him. She looked at Ellie, "What now then?"

Ellie looked back, "First, how are you feeling?" her face showed a lot of sympathy and support, the question felt genuine.

Emilia smiled, "Better, but still like I have been hit by a bus or something."

"It looked like quite a fall; I'm surprised that energy thing worked though."

Emilia sat down on the floor, a strange sensation as it was moving and flowing in the same way as the walls that surrounded them. Ellie did the same and immediately had the same thoughts, neither of them had ever paid much attention to this place, they had always been preoccupied.

"You need to get your energy back; do you feel any different?" Ellie asked.

"Actually, I do," Emilia admitted. "Whatever you did is certainly helping, I can sense the feeling coming back in my legs and everything."

"Good. I think that could be more down to being here though. When we are here, we are more spirit form than anything else. Would certainly explain why he is so much stronger here."

Emilia nodded, "There is one thing I don't get though."

Ellie looked at her.

"How did you do it? How is it you can control the energy and stuff? I know I can't."

Ellie sighed, "I honestly don't really understand either, all I do know is that I have only been able to since he trapped me here and did what he did."

"What did he do?"

"You don't know?" Ellie asked, a little confused. "I thought he had told you everything?"

Emilia shook her head, "Well he told me everything he wanted to tell me. He told me he made me so that I would help him. That he had created me to do exactly as he needed me to do."

Ellie looked down, "That is all true, he did make you. From me."

The two girls looked at each other, their eyes meeting for the first time since they met on the hill by the statue.

Ellie continued, solemnly, "He trapped me here, tied me up, and pulled my spirit out, so I know how that feels. I had the energy pulled out of me like you have right now. He did something called a splice, he split my spirit energy in two, and gave me back part then created you from the other by throwing it into my timeline. Apparently, he kept the bits that he wanted to in you that allow him to make you do what he wanted to do."

"Like being angry, resentful, stubborn, and stupid?" Emilia admitted.

Ellie chuckled, "Don't be too hard on yourself, you didn't know. Besides he planned all this out, not like he made it up on the spot or anything." She took Emilia's hand, "He tricked me before as well," she smiled kindly.

"So, what do we do? How do we beat him?"

"That's a good question," Ellie said, standing as she did so. "We need to find him and see if there is something he missed, another mistake. He didn't mean to give me the ability to use the energy flow so maybe he made another mistake somewhere?"

"Ok, how do we do that?" Emilia asked, impatience beginning to show.

Ellie thought and looked around. Everywhere was purple, everywhere was also moving and it was beginning to make her feel sick. "Ok, he is here somewhere, he must be, with your spirit energy and that is what he wants to use. So, we find him, get your spirit back to you, and then work out what's next. Good plan?" Ellie stuck her thumbs up in a mocking positive team spirit sort of way.

Emilia laughed, standing as she did so, "Ok, I'm in. And feeling better. Lead and I'll follow."

"Ok, not sure where I can lead you to though."

"Maybe you can trace him or something?" Emilia asked hopefully.

Ellie looked at her with a raised eyebrow, "You have a lot of faith in me suddenly, but ok I'll give it a go."

She closed her eyes and tried to feel what was around her. The problem was, there was nothing around her. No sounds, nothing to feel, or sense. She thought about the Man, what he looked like, how he moved and talked.

"Where are you?" Ellie asked out loud softly.

Nothing.

"Where are you?" both girls asked at the same time, confident but not too bold.

"Now this is a surprise, too little too late, but a surprise none the less," came the soft voice of the Man that filled them both with dread. "Eleanor can sense me I'm sure, come and look, you are too late though I'm afraid."

Within seconds the purple vapour disappeared, and the two girls were back on the hilltop once more, except it was daylight and clear. They looked around and could see nothing but rolling green hills for miles.

"Where are we?" Emilia asked.

Ellie had turned away and was walking towards an alcove of rock, it had drawings on it, markings. She looked all around beginning to piece it together, "I think I know," she said, turning to face Emilia.

"Care to share?"

"I think I have been here before; this is the time of the first council. This bit of land right here is where the Statue Of Mow will be. This, is the home of Abijah."

"Well done," came the Man's voice. The girls turned to face where it was coming from, there he was, floating and glowing as always. "So, you found me, but have you figured out why we are here and what is going to happen?"

The girls looked at each other, neither wanting to be the first to speak.

"I did not think so, you see, you never really understood what this was did you Eleanor?"

"What do you mean? It is just a vision you are showing us like you did to me before."

"Right before you took her soul to make me only to take it back again," Emilia added.

"Well done, Emilia. Eleanor, try harder. What makes you think this is a vision?"

"You told me it was, when I was here before when you left me here," Ellie answered, confused.

"Yes I did, when you were here before it was a recreation."

Ellie went to reply, then stopped herself, thinking.

"Now you are getting it," he gloated.

"This is real?" Ellie exclaimed, panic setting in a little.

"What?" Emilia chimed in. "You have sent us back in time?"

He said nothing, just floated there silently.

"Say something," Emilia demanded.

"Eleanor, what you saw before was a recreation, but it will match this perfectly. This is real, so I would be very careful what you do if I were you," he started to fade away. "You may find that you make things worse for yourselves."

"You can't just leave us here," Ellie implored, but it was too late, he had gone.

The girls looked at each other.

"Now what?" Emilia asked. "He said this will match what you saw before except that this is real so what happens next?"

Ellie thought, "So he sent me here before and I could touch the ground and trees and stuff, but nobody could hear or see me." She headed to the alcove and found the round stone with the symbol of Mow, "I fell over this, tripped over it, which is when I knew it was a little more than a vision."

Emilia went and looked, "Ok, you fell over, then what?"

"Then I saw Abijah, I tried to hide from him but fell again as I ran towards that tree."

"You need to learn not to fall over," Emilia joked.

"Thanks, but maybe after we figure this out," she knelt and looked at the stone. "We need to hide, now," she stated, standing, and looking at Emilia with panic in her eyes.

"Why?"

"If this is real and people can see us then we cannot be found like this."

She grabbed Emilia's arm and dragged her over to the tree she was running towards last time she was here. After a few seconds they were there, panting but hiding from sight.

"Why the panic?" Emilia asked confused.

"Abijah is about to appear over that hill, then he will start chanting until the Man appears. This is the day that he reveals himself to the first council. He basically tricks them into building him the folly. They believe him to be a god that is going to save them."

"When he actually wants to use it to destroy us?" Emilia confirmed.

Ellie nodded.

"So, what are we looking for and how do we get out of here?"

"I don't think we want to get out of here, not yet."

Emilia looked at her.

"Think about it. The original Man is here and will do what he needs to do to get the folly built, the same as what I saw the last time yes?"

Emilia nodded.

"But the Man from our time is here too with your spirit energy, he must want to do something with it now that will mean in the future, he can use it to destroy the barrier between the worlds."

Emilia's eyes widened, "So, you want to find our Man, and stay out of the way of the original Man, and all the locals?"

Ellie nodded, "Pretty much. Unless you have a better idea?"

Emilia said nothing.

"Ok, we need to find him," Ellie stated confidently. She peered round the tree, back towards Abijah's rock. He was there now facing the other way.

"What happens next?" Emilia asked.

"He starts bowing and praying to the Man-" Ellie stopped, grabbed Emilia by the arm and dragged her further into the trees.

"Hey," Emilia started to shout before Ellie covered her mouth with her hand.

"Shhhhhhhh," she nodded through the trees.

Floating not that far away was the Man, the original Man that Abijah was about to start bowing to. Ellie let Emilia go and they both stared at him as he moved through the trees towards Abijah.

The girls watched and waited, it played out exactly how Ellie remembered it, right up until Abijah left the hilltop and the Man disappeared.

"I followed Abijah last time," Ellie said, "Well, when it was a recreation I mean."

"Where did he go?"

"He went around the village, speaking to the other council

members, checking on the keys and stuff. Tonight is the night that the keys get joined together through the Earth and all the rocks and stones appeared to make the folly."

"So, this is where it all begins?"

"I guess so," Ellie said as she sat down on the ground. "So, what is our Man doing back here, what is he going to do?"

Emilia sat next to her, "Something that involves my spirit but would not interfere with what happened before."

"Yes, he has been very clear that he needs everything that has already happened to happen in the same way."

"Would that even work?" Emilia asked. "I always thought if you made a change it would change everything?"

"Unless it was a subtle change maybe," Ellie commented. "What would be small enough that nobody would notice?"

They sat and thought until eventually Emilia spoke, "Tonight is the night that he comes across as super god Man yeah?"

Ellie chuckled, "Yes, he flies over the hill and sends bolts of light all over the place joining the stones together. It is also the night that the first council is terrified into making up all those crazy rules."

"So, the old Man is going to be with Abijah and the villagers on the hilltop."

Ellie nodded.

"That leaves this place, where the Statue Of Mow will be, empty. I bet that is where our Man will be tonight."

They looked at each other.

"Makes sense I guess," Ellie commented. "So, we wait here then?"

"At least we won't get seen up here," Emilia stated.

They made themselves comfortable on the ground and settled down to wait for nightfall.

A little while later, Emilia woke with a start. It was almost dark and until now she was not aware they had fallen asleep. It took a moment for her to get her bearings again, and most importantly to work out what had woken her. Voices. She could hear voices not too far away, she nudged Ellie to wake her.

"Hey," she whispered, "someone's coming."

Ellie woke instantly and sat bolt upright.

Emilia looked around the tree, "I can't see anyone, but I can definitely hear someone though."

The girls looked up the hill, then they both saw the sources of the voices. A man and woman were walking up the hill in the twilight, they were heading towards the place where the statue would eventually be. Emilia moved to get a little closer, Ellie followed.

"That's Thomas and Isabella," Ellie whispered. "Two members of the first council."

Emilia nodded in understanding.

They moved closer still, keeping to the trees and moving as quietly as possible, eventually they were close enough to overhear what they were saying.

"So, you still think he is making it up?" Thomas asked.

"I don't know," Isabella replied, "I just think it's strange that it's all happening and that he is the only one that can see this Man Of Mow."

"That is odd I agree. He has always been the one that has kept us in touch with the spirit side of things though."

Ellie tapped Emilia on the shoulder, then whispered, "They were arguing earlier, she thinks that Abijah is making it up as an excuse for not wanting a daughter. The girl that was sacrificed is the daughter of Abijah and Elizabeth."

"Wow, that's messed up," Emilia exclaimed as loudly as she dared but keeping a low profile behind the trees.

They looked back at the two villagers, they had paused by the location of the future statue.

"Why is he living here? Why doesn't he stay at home with Elizabeth and the baby?"

"No idea," Thomas replied. "Best view on the hill, but he claims it is where he sees the Man and where he is learning what we need to do to safeguard our future."

"Well, I hope he is right, and all this is worth it."

With that the two headed away along the path.

"They are going to the folly site, that is where I was last time, I watched from the hilltop," Ellie stated.

"Still no sign of our Man showing up is there, how do we know if we are in the right place?"

"We don't," Ellie admitted. "We are making this up as we go along really aren't we. The stuff with the hilltop and the stones doesn't happen until midnight though, so if it is related to that we have a while to wait."

They looked at each other, both waiting for the other to say something.

"I'm trying to remember what happened, when I saw it all earlier," Ellie finally said.

Emilia looked at her. "What do you mean?"

"I must have missed something; I was focused on the hill of course but there must be something. I remember waiting on the hilltop, knowing that they couldn't see me made this much easier. The council gathered on the hilltop looking at the very peak, you know the bit where the folly is today."

Emilia nodded.

"They sat there looking up like they were about to watch fireworks or something. I sat on top of the hill, so I was between the Man and the council."

"What did he do?"

"He played god. He appeared to them, floated above the hill and made himself look like an angel or something. Lightning came down from the sky, through him and into the ground. He said he was joining the stones with power. As he did all this the ground shook and moved as the rocks appeared all over the hill."

"So, the five keys are joined together, they meet under the folly?"

"I guess so, they also join up using the energy flow remember as well, the five stones send five beams up to the folly constantly. The folly just focuses it."

"What I don't understand," Emilia began, "Is if he did all this to create something to destroy the barrier but got it wrong, yeah?"

"Yes."

"And the folly simply channels the energy and helped focus it. What's the statue all about?" She looked at the place where it would be, "Where does that fit in with all this?"

Ellie's eyes widened, "He mentioned it. He made it as a sort of back door into the prison realm, that's how he escaped this

time."
Emilia looked back at her, "What?"
"When he trapped me, after I had touched the statue, he told me that this was his back door, he asked Abijah and the villagers to place the stones in such a way that there would be a back door in case his folly idea didn't work. Kind of like a stage door to a theatre, not fancy or anything but functional. All he needed was me to touch it with my palm for it to open."
"Why your palm?" Emilia looked confused, "Surely that would just be like touching any other stone?"
"Unless he did something to it now, meaning it would react to someone specific? I've never touched it before so can't really tell or know."
They both looked at the alcove, imagining the pile of rocks that would become the Statue Of Mow. As they watched, they could see a pool of light appearing on the crest of the hill, just out of sight.
"Looks like he is by the folly site, whatever happens will happen soon," Ellie stated.
Emilia decided to take control, "Let's move to get a better view, they will all be up there now, so we should be ok."
The girls moved along the path to give themselves a clear view of the future statue site. Not long after they found a spot not too far away, the sky was filled with a brilliant white light. It was as if the hill was the support for a giant lamp that had just been turned on; it lit up everything with a pure saturating light. The ground shook and vibrated, Ellie and Emilia supported each other as they leant on the tree they were hiding behind, though this was vibrating also. They peered around towards the statue site. Pushing up out of the ground, twisting and turning as it did was the statue they recognised. First the head stone; shaped and carving itself from a larger stone, this was then pushed into the air by what would be the body. When this was completely above ground the pieces that formed the basic shape of his shoulders forced their way to its side and seemed to fuse with the stone body. More stone, each piece pushing the previous one higher until eventually it was at full height. The Statue Of Mow. The ground continued to shake and as they watched, the Man appeared and moved towards the newly formed statue.

They knew it was the one from their time as following close behind was Emilia's spirit form. The girls took a chance and moved out from behind the tree that had sheltered them. The Man had arrived at the statue now and had positioned the yellow glow of Emilia's spirit between the statue and himself. He put up his palms in front of him as if defending himself from it, over the noise of the ground shaking they could just make out his words.

"I embed you in this stone, to observe for all time. To wait for the touch of that which is your match. You shall remain here until I release you. If the touch of your match should occur, you will let them through, and I shall know. You are mine to command and your power is mine to control."

There was a deafening bang, it seemed to come from two places at once. The hilltop by the folly and here by the statue, the girls turned and hid once more.

"He timed that so nobody would notice, they are all focused on the Man from here and now, he can do what he likes here," Ellie said as loudly as she dared.

Emilia nodded in agreement.

As they watched, the yellow glow faded as Emilia's spirit pushed back into the rock and vanished from view. Moments later, the Man they had been watching moved through the same stone and presumably back to their real time.

They crept out once more.

"Now what?" Ellie asked.

Emilia headed towards the statue, "How long before the Man comes around here do you think?"

"What?"

You said earlier that after the hilltop he comes here to check on the statue; how much time do we have?"

"Minutes, maybe five or ten," Ellie tried to recall.

"Ok, then come quick I have an idea."

They jogged over to the statue and stopped in front of the rock that the spirit had been forced into.

"The one that I touched, that gave me this mark is the one he put your spirit in," Ellie stated.

"Well at least we know why that works the way it does now."

"Do we?" Ellie asked, confused.

"Didn't you hear him? He said that if the touch of your match should occur then let them through. You are its match, it is spirit made from you. He set that trap way in advance."

Ellie was hit with this realisation as though she had run into the rock headfirst, "Ok, so what do you think we can do about it?"

Emilia said nothing.

Ellie continued, "What if he made another mistake? His whole idea was that we would not work together, that you would be the opposite of me, what if we both touched it at the same time?"

They looked at each other, then with a shrug Emilia stepped forward, "Ok, on three?"

Ellie found the spot where she thought she'd touched it for the first time and hovered her hand over it. She looked at Emilia, "You find a spot and memorise it; we may need it to find it again."

Emilia did so and then hovered her hand above the surface of the rock as well.

"One."

"Two."

"Three."

The girls counted together and on the strike of three both placed their hand on the rock. There was a flash of golden yellow and everything vanished, leaving them in what appeared to be an empty space. There was nothing between them and nothing around them. They stood, confused. As they looked at each other a faint orange glow began to emerge between them, the same way that a candle glows when first lit with a match. They stepped back as the glow got larger and filled their faces with light until they realised what it was. They were looking at the spirit energy of Emilia. It had plain features but was Emilia, it turned its blank looking face first to Ellie then to Emilia.

"How can I serve you?" it said in a voice that was identical to Emilia's.

The two girls looked at each other, speechless.

It spoke once more, "You are my match; how can I serve you?"

Emilia broke the silence, "How is this possible? What is happening?"

"I was created and placed with specific instructions, but you acted in a way that was not part of those instructions. Therefore, my spirit will allow new ones to be created overruling the first."

"We can use you to help us?"

"Correct, I will do your bidding."

Emilia looked at Ellie, eyes wide with hope, "Do you trust me?"

Ellie looked at her for a moment, "Yes," she said softly.

Emilia smiled then looked back at the spirit, "I would like the previous instructions to stand."

"What?" Ellie interrupted, Emilia shot her a look, "Sorry, carry on," she immediately backed down though was a little concerned at this point.

"I would like the previous instructions to stand until you sense the touch of your match twice, both of us, like just now."

The spirit said nothing.

"Then, I would like you to absorb anything that is spirit based, including us, into the prison realm between worlds. Can you do that?"

"I can, I will absorb anything that is near me that is not from your world into the prison realm."

"And us too," Ellie added, understanding what Emilia was planning.

Emilia looked at her and smiled, "Yes, us as well. Then we want your power to be dispersed into the area around you."

"Understood. Now, you must return," the spirit stated.

With a blinding flash, the girls found themselves standing by the rock at the foot of the Statue Of Mow. It was glowing a faint purple but was as it should be as far as they could tell.

They looked at each other, then turned and ran back up the path to hide once more. They got there just in time. As soon as they got there the Man appeared floating down the path towards the statue. They could hear him muttering to himself.

"On the first full moon I will use the pure child's energy to rip open the portal and absorb all the energy from this miserable world into my own."

Ellie moved slightly to get a better view.

He carried on, "They won't get a chance to build that stupid folly, Abijah believes he is their saviour when really he has-"

Ellie stepped too far and caused a twig on the ground to crack, the Man cut short his chatter and turned to face in their direction. The girls froze. They were quite far back, and Ellie was pretty sure that he could not see them, but she did not dare move.

Then he spoke again, "I see you; I do not know you, but I see you. I know I cannot deal with you now, but no matter, even if you are here you cannot stop me now," he turned and continued up the path.

Ellie let out a sigh of relief, "I'm an idiot. I saw that before; I saw him say that to this very tree when this was recreated as a vision."

She moved back behind the tree with Emilia.

"You saw us before?"

"No, not us, just the trees. At the time I thought he was talking to me, I just didn't remember it happening. Sorry."

"We got away with it, that's what counts. We made a change that he doesn't know about and now we have a fighting chance. Let's get out of here."

They smiled and together headed down the now empty path towards the Statue Of Mow. They reached the stone.

"One at a time?" Emilia stated, "Don't need our rabbit out of the hat yet. You go first." Ellie smiled and walked up to the stone, putting her hand on it and vanishing in a flash of purple.

Emilia looked round, taking a moment to saviour the peace and quiet. She had a bad feeling about what was coming. It scared her, not knowing what it was all she could do was carry on, but she knew that there was something on the horizon for her. After a few moments she too approached the stone and placed her palm on the surface.

CHAPTER 13

Ellie.

Ellie was used to the feeling of being moved around through these stones, the feeling of being pulled from behind the stomach had been a new one at first, but now she barely noticed it. There was also something special about this particular arrival here; in the prison realm, the space between worlds. This was the first time she had arrived here feeling confident, as though she was in charge and had the upper hand. Looking around she was greeted by the same flowing, moving purple walls, ceiling, and floor. Even the sight of the vapour like smoke did not phase her this time. Ellie knew that any second Emilia would be with her and they would be able to make the next move before the Man got anywhere near them or their plan. She took a few steps forward, although here there was no difference between forwards and backwards as everywhere was the same. Purple.

"I wonder why it is purple?" Ellie asked out loud without really thinking about it.

"Purple inspires deeper thoughts, connects the spiritual, and the physical," a soft voice answered her.

Ellie looked around, there was nobody there, but she recognised the voice, "You designed it, then did you?" she asked of the Man.

"Indeed, I added the colour. Remember this was not designed as a place to keep me incarcerated, it was originally designed as a bridge between your world and Imaginari."

This was of little comfort to Ellie, she wanted and needed Emilia by her side, so they could tackle this together, head on as they had planned.

The Man continued, still hidden from view, "It was designed as a way for my world to reach yours, and to allow us to travel through it. When we first created it, we worked together. I suggested the colour to allow us to be as creative and open minded as possible. I felt that when you have no physical form, being able to keep your mind creative and active is of even more importance. Purple helps with this and allows for calmer emotions whilst you are creating and thinking."

"Believe me, I am calm, but in a way that you will not like," Ellie retorted sharply.

"This is very interesting, where has this new-found confidence and strength come from I wonder? It is misplaced of course but I am intrigued."

Ellie considered this, she was not sure how much she should talk about or reveal, they needed him back in the real world first. She decided to try and buy some time. "After I had a conversation with someone that knows you, someone that wants to stop you but can't."

He chuckled, "You mean those fools that could not think big enough? The ones who call themselves Guardians when in fact they are just happy to watch things decay over thousands of years?"

Ellie fidgeted slightly but said nothing.

"It is true that I was once like them, we were all from the same world and we all wanted to ensure that world would continue. Our world is a peaceful one but as I have said to you before, a world without form is very difficult to live in, especially when you have experienced the physicality of your world. This is not the first time they have interfered, but I have learned my lesson and they will not stop me again."

"They stopped you before?" Ellie asked, feeling like she was learning more now than she ever had about this.

"Yes. A long time ago before humans had begun to cover the Earth, I tried to carry out my scheme. Alas, the creatures that were here then could not help me to do what I needed to do. They were not capable of complex thought or reason and so could not build me anything, be influenced by me, or help me at all. I still tried to carry out my plan, but this coupled with the Guardians interference led to the temporary destruction of the Guardians, and me. Or so they thought."

"I feel like you are enjoying gloating over me, so carry on. Tell me what happened, all of it."

She knew she was taking a risk here; would he carry on talking long enough?

"Very well, I will tell you because you cannot stop me now, it is too late. My world first discovered yours and soon after we realised that the energy flow from yours was sustaining ours. We wanted to understand how it worked and if there was a way we could make our world better. There were five of us, we pulled as much energy as we could and forced ourselves through a touch point between worlds and arrived in yours. We were greeted with sights, sounds, and the knowledge of physical contact. We wanted it for our world, we wanted what the creatures had, so we set about seeing if we could do so. We worked together at first and opened a gateway into our world from yours. It took all five of us to do it and we soon realised that what we were doing would destroy your world. The other four tried to stop, but I resisted, I wanted to carry on and get as much as we could. They sacrificed themselves to stop me and we were scattered, but there were still consequences."

"Consequences? For who?"

"Everyone. The four who tried to stop me dissolved their forms like mine and were turned to vapour in your physical world. They are trapped like that now stuck in a cycle between liquid and gas. I absorbed most of their power and over time this is what has allowed me to show myself to you and begin my plans once more. I was trapped in my world unable to return for millennia. The biggest price paid however, was paid by your world. The explosion of energy from the point of the gateway caused it to collapse in on itself, sending a shockwave of power across the sky and into the Earth. It tore the sky apart, sent rivers of fire across the surface, and turned the sky black. Nearly all life on Earth was wiped out, I had to wait not only for my strength to return but also for life in your physical world to be strong enough to sustain the energy flow once more. Our world was weakened, I was weakened, all I could do was think and plan."

Ellie listened, open mouthed with amazement, "How long ago did this happen? You said millennia?"

"Yes, the event happened around sixty-five million years ago, yet I have only been able to bring myself into your world within the last few thousand years, exploring, trying to find a way to carry out my plan, now I have done just that."

"You're talking about the dinosaurs? You're telling me that the thing that wiped out the dinosaurs was you trying to steal the energy from our world? And you still think it's a good idea?"

"Yes, you are correct, and yes I do. I believe your world has had more than its fair share of chances. My world deserves all the chances now. That is what I have been working on, that is what I have been planning, and you will not stop me."

Ellie could not quite process this, but it did give her a very clear picture of what would happen if they failed. She knew that nobody had ever been able to confirm what wiped out the dinosaurs, but she also knew that rivers of lava and black skies filled with ash were not a good thing.

"It's not over yet," she retorted with more strength than she thought she had at this point.

"Yes, it is. I have done something that you cannot deal with, and you are here alone once more at my mercy. What has changed that makes you think otherwise?"

"I can manipulate the energy flow; I can see it and use it."

"I know you can, an unexpected side effect I admit but I am not concerned by this, for what I have done has been in place for thousands of years, building and building so that it can do what I need it to do."

"And what is that exactly?"

"It will produce the same amount of energy, more even, than the four spirits I had with me. No folly to help, no special stones or the like. Just power, raw, untamed, near unlimited power to tear the barriers apart."

There was a snarl in his voice now, it made Ellie feel very small and alone.

"I won't stop," she said, a little weaker this time.

The Man formed a short distance away, floating in front of Ellie, "I know you won't, but you cannot stop me, Eleanor Fields."

Ellie squared her shoulders up to face him head on but before she could say anything another voice spoke from behind her. "Yes, we can."

Ellie did not need to look, she just smiled at him, not even blinking.

From behind her Emilia appeared, "We are going to stop you. Because we have a plan as well, and I am willing to bet you were not ready to see us together today."

Emilia walked around Ellie and stood to her right; the two girls were now side by side staring at the Man defiantly. Ellie had never felt such a surge of confidence as when she heard Emilia's voice; she was not alone. That thought was enough to push her on and gave her the strength she needed to stay standing firm.

"What did I miss?" Emilia asked sweetly.

"Nothing really, the usual gloating," Ellie replied, still looking directly at the Man. "He is going on about how he did this before and killed the dinosaurs so there is one mystery solved."

They had not spoken of or agreed to any kind of plan that meant antagonising him or indeed pushing him too far. It came so naturally to them though that they carried on, fully intent on pushing him to make a mistake.

"No way," Emilia commented sarcastically, "That means we know more about the dinosaurs than anyone who has ever lived. Cheers pal," she stuck her thumb up to him.

"Silence," he shouted, and they immediately focused back on him once more. "This is not a game, this is destiny."

"See, the thing is," Ellie interrupted. "We have both heard you give your speeches over and over before and they are just a bit, well, boring."

"Yes, that's exactly it," Emilia agreed. "It's all very bland."

"I can see the mistake I made," came the soft reply.

"Yeup, you allowed us to get to know each other," Ellie confirmed. "Should have kept us apart but couldn't help but

try and watch us hurt each other though, could you?"
He looked at them both, first at Ellie, then Emilia, and then back to Ellie again.
"Indeed, I wanted you to suffer and watch you toil in torment and pain," he snarled. "But it does not matter that you are together, the damage is already done, and you cannot change what I did nor what is going to happen."
"See, I think we can," Ellie interrupted once more. "I think the very fact that we are here together is going against your plan and your scheme, and that means we have a chance."
Emilia nodded in agreement, "And whilst there is a chance, we won't give up."
The girls leant into each-other, so their shoulders nudged, it was not a strong statement of teamwork, but it was enough of a sign of solidarity to infuriate the Man.
"Enough," he shouted, and as he did he slammed his hands together in a loud clap. As he did so a burst of invisible energy shot out from his hands towards the girls. Before they could react, it had reached them and blasted them apart sending them sprawling over the purple pulsating floor. Ellie tried to roll with the impact of the ground to get back to her feet but before she could golden strands of light had appeared once more and bound her legs to the floor. No sooner had she realised this, then her hands were also bound behind her. She was tied on her knees; hands being pulled behind her and forcing her body into a strict upright position meaning she could barely move. To her horror, Emilia was in the same predicament opposite her, the two girls were facing each other as an almost perfect mirror image. Both bound, both unable to move.
"That's better," The Man gloated as he moved to float between them. "You will soon learn that this is your natural place, kneeling before me and accepting your fate. I have worked too hard and planned for too long to watch this fall apart now and you will not stop me."
Silence. Then a small chuckle of laughter spilled out of Ellie's mouth. She did not mean too, but once it had arrived, she could not stop it and before long she was chuckling away to herself.

The Man turned to face her and lowered himself to her eye height, "What is so funny?"

"Nothing, it's just, well. You say how powerful you are and how your plan is going to work, and we cannot stop it. But…" she paused to let a small chuckle out. "But, you can't carry out this plan without tying up a couple of girls and gloating over them. I just think it is strange is all," she laughed some more. To Ellie's delight, Emilia was also chuckling away to herself, she was glad that they were both on the same wavelength. They had not had chance to discuss it, but Ellie knew they had to get back to the real world with the Man, so they could touch the stone together. That was their only hope, and they could only do that if he came back with them. After listening to him talk to her she had decided that the best way to do this was infuriate him to the point of wanting to gloat over everyone.

"I can do this without stopping you, you are just an irritation that I do not need," he defended.

"Prove it then," Ellie said, staring at him with a piercing stare. "Prove to us that you are worthy of our fear."

If he could blink, Ellie was sure that he would have then. He rose to his full height once more and turned to face Emilia.

"I would have expected this attitude from you, after all I created you to be so bitter and angry."

"Well, we are the same person," Emilia defied him. "You just tried to meddle in things that you didn't understand."

This seemed to do the trick. The Man moved so quickly that he was almost a blur to be right in front of Emilia's face.

"You think I do not understand? You think that I do not know what pain and suffering is like? You have no idea what I am capable of girl, you are merely days old with fake memories that I gave you from her," he pointed at Ellie.

"I have a name," Ellie added.

"Silence," he snarled without looking at her. "I will show you both what I can do, I will make sure that as your world burns you are not only powerless to stop it, but that you are the last two humans alive. You will watch as your entire civilisation falls in the knowledge that it was your fault."

He moved away from Emilia and rose, turning so the girls

were now side on to him. He lifted his arms out sideways slowly as he did so. Ellie took the chance to glance at Emilia who had done the exact same thing. They shared a knowing nod that they were in agreement and so far, everything was working the way they had hoped and wanted it to.

"I shall reveal myself to the world, your world, and then we shall watch it burn from the hill in Mow Cop together."

He raised his hands above his head then brought them slamming down against his sides. As they hit there was a blinding flash and both girls closed their eyes to shield them from the light. Ellie opened her eyes and first checked that Emilia was still there, she was. A shocked look on her face but she was there all the same. What was different though was the surroundings, Ellie was now aware of a breeze, and grass beneath her knees. She was still bound and unable to move but she could turn her head. As she did so she heard a voice calling out to them both.

"Emilia, Ellie."

Then she realised it was not a voice, it was lots of voices, she was greeted by looks of horror and fear on the faces of her friends. They were back by the Statue Of Mow, as far as she could tell just moments after they had left.

There was a moment when nobody said anything, then this was broken by Annabelle's panicked tone.

"Emilia, Ellie. What happened? You were there one second then you appeared here like this, kneeling facing each other. What is going on?"

She walked towards them but was butted away by an invisible barrier. She put out her hands to touch it and immediately felt a force against her palm. She hit it, nothing. Seeing her panicked expression, the others hurried over and they too could not find a way past whatever was keeping them back. Ellie looked around and was puzzled by the fact that she could still not move but there did not appear to be anything holding her in place. Looking at Emilia, she seemed to be having the same thoughts. They looked at each other, confusion etched across their faces. They struggled against their invisible bonds and their friends hammered away at what was keeping them back, but nothing changed or gave way. Then there was an Earth-shattering cackle, followed by a voice that was all too familiar to Ellie and Emilia.

"Now is this not more like it," boomed the Man's voice. But to Ellie's surprise, her friends stopped banging and shouting, it appeared they too could hear him this time. "Watching all of you struggle and battle against something that you cannot see or understand is very amusing I must say."

"Where are you?" Emilia shouted.

"Who is that?" came Simon's voice, sounding more scared than Ellie had ever heard him before.

"Why Simon Lesley, it is I, the Man Of Mow."

"How do you know my name?"

More chuckles, "I know everything there is to know about you, and this pesky little village."

"What do you want?" Annabelle asked, clearly believing that this voice was new to everybody.

"I want to destroy your world. Your friends here, Eleanor and Emilia, have helped me."

"They would never help you."

"Well, they have. And soon they will watch as the world burns and every living thing in it perishes to dust as my world thrives."

"Still scared to show yourself properly, though aren't you?" Ellie chimed in, getting some of her strength back, winking at Emilia as she did so.

"On the contrary, I intend to reveal myself to you all."

As he spoke there was a pure white brilliant light. It started out as a sphere about the size of a tennis ball floating in the air and got brighter and brighter. The group of friends moved back, shielding their eyes from the light. Ellie and Emilia could only close their eyes as their hands were still bound behind them. The sphere grew, stretching itself longer and longer in mid-air until eventually it formed the shape of the Man. Floating in the air facing out over the hill surveying all that was before him.

"This is me," he boomed. "You will watch as your world burns."

He glided down towards the group, aiming directly for

Annabelle.

"You leave them alone," Ellie called out, struggling against her bonds that would not yield any slack at all.

He chuckled, "I will not harm them, do not worry." He reached out a hand and cupped it around Annabelle's face, "Such a pretty girl, I can see why you both like her so much," he taunted.

"Get away from me," Annabelle hissed.

"You show bravery when confronted with me, good, I like that. It will be fun to watch you all perish." He turned and moved back towards the statue, "Now you will all see my victory, and you, Eleanor Fields, will be the last one left alive. You will watch from right here, powerless to stop me."

Ellie struggled against her bonds again, they would not break. She knew they needed a plan, something that would allow them to get free. All they had to do was make it to the rock together and touch it at the same time. But how? Before she could think about this too much, it started.

The Man had reached the rock, the rock that the girls knew contained the spirit of Emilia and placed his hands on it. As he did so there was an almighty bang and the Earth shook bringing the group of friends to their knees with the vibration. Ellie and Emilia could do nothing but watch in fear. The golden glow of Emilia's spirit came out of the stone, but it was different now, different to the one they had seen in the past. It was fuller somehow, it looked stronger and bolder. Ellie looked at it with confusion and fear.

"Impressive," The Man gloated, looking over his creation. "You have absorbed more than I could ever have imagined," he turned to face the girls. "You see, your spirit Emilia, taken from that of Eleanor, has been here for thousands of years. It has absorbed all the negative energy that has been within a thousand miles for centuries. It has grown in strength and will soon be ready for me to use to destroy the gateway between our worlds. This will create a vacuum that will suck all the energy from everything that is living in your world and reduce it to ash. All it needs is one final thing."

The girls looked at each other, confused as to what was about to happen.

"What do you mean?" Emilia asked.

He turned to face her, "It is true this is your spirit and no doubt you are now starting to feel weaker now that you are in your physical world?"

It was true, Ellie could see the colour had drained from Emilia's face and she seemed to be struggling for breath once more. "Emilia, don't listen to him, stay strong," she encouraged.

"I'm afraid it is too late for that, girl. As you know you cannot survive without your spirit form and Emilia's has been removed for some time now. She will fade soon. But as I was saying this spirit needs one final thing." He moved over to Emilia, who struggled weakly against her bonds, but it was no use she could not escape or move away from him as he approached. "It simply needs something of yours, a strand of hair will suffice."

"My hair?" Emilia asked confused.

"Yes, to complete the circle and close all the loops it needs physical contact with your DNA once again. This will reverse the flow and instead of absorbing all the negative energy, it will expel it in one go."

He reached out a bony hand towards Emilia's head.

"But, you can't touch anything physical from our world, can you?"

"I can if I try hard enough, it will weaken me, but I think I can take that risk."

He paused with his fingers almost at Emilia's head, as he did so Ellie noticed his hand seem to shimmer and shine brighter than the rest of his body. By contrast the rest of his body faded slightly, he appeared to be sending as much energy as he could to his hand from everywhere else, as if sacrificing it all to allow this one moment of physical contact. He reached out and plucked a single golden hair from Emilia's head. She did not react, seemingly too weak to even notice as she was now only being held up by her restraints. The Man turned and moved back towards the glowing spirit in front of the rock. He too seemed weaker now in the way he moved, focusing all his energy on the one hand holding the single golden hair. When he reached it, he gently lifted his hand above the spirit and released the hair. It fell through the air in what felt like slow motion until it reached the floating head of the golden spirit. The moment it made contact, everything seemed to happen at once. First there was a flash of light, with the golden spirit at its centre that shot out across the sky like lightning. As it passed over hills, trees, and houses it gave out a brilliant light as if the sun had been turned on then off again seconds later. At that moment, Emilia's bonds were released, and she fell to the floor in a heap, Ellie's remained strong though and she was unable to go to her aid. The group of friends were blasted back across the floor by the flash of light, which seemingly carried force with it as well. The earth began to vibrate and shimmer once more. The Man and the golden spirit began to float upwards, above the height of the statue and into the sky, as it did so the spirit seemed to grow in brightness. Once they reached a height that meant there were above everything, the hilltop, the folly, all of it, the golden spirit shot into the sky like a firework, leaving a golden trail of light behind it. Ellie guessed it was aiming for the gateway above the folly, when it got to the weakness between worlds it seemed to explode, leaving behind a huge black hole in between the swirling black clouds. She stared at the hole, it was correct to say it was black, but it was so black it seemed to be non-existent, as if all light seemed to fall into it and immediately vanish into darkness.

"And now it begins," the Man called down over the noise of the wind, vibrating earth, and screams of fear from the group on the hill.

To Ellie's surprise, the next thing to happen was that her bonds released and she fell forwards onto the floor. She took a moment to see if the Man had noticed but he was too busy admiring the view above him. First, she looked at the group of friends, but they too were fixated by the swirling vortex above them. So, she crawled over to where Emilia was lying and tried to rouse her.

"Emilia, come on, we need to move now," but there was no reply, Emilia was out cold and was showing no signs of life. Ellie turned her over onto her back and checked her pulse, it was weak, but it was there.

"Ellie, get out of there," Annabelle called above the deafening wind. "It's getting worse," she pointed up.

Ellie looked up at the sky again. The black hole had spread and was now seemingly pulling everything near it inwards. She could not see the energy or spirits being pulled, but she was aware of the impact. On the hilltop around her the grass was starting to wilt and the trees were losing their leaves, all as if having the life pulled out of them by the hole in the sky.

"I can't, I need to stop him," she called back. "We, need to."

She looked at Annabelle, and for the first time felt connected to her in the same way as she remembered. The two girls locked eyes, and in that moment, they knew the truth of what was about to happen. Tears formed on Annabelle's face as Ellie struggled to her feet and hauled Emilia onto her back. She took one last look at Annabelle and then turned back towards the stone. One long struggling step at a time she forced herself towards it, fighting to keep her balance on the shaking earth and not get blown away by the gale force winds. She glanced up and immediately wished she had not, the sight was demoralising. The black hole had spread and had now covered the top of the hill and the surrounding village, it was clear to Ellie that this is how it would work, spreading darkness and absorbing all life until the whole planet was consumed by it. She got closer to the stone, three steps to go, two to go, one. She lowered herself and sat Emilia as best she could on the floor by the stone. She grabbed hold of Emilia's wrist in her left hand and lined it as best she could with where she thought she had touched it before. Then she positioned herself so that she could place her right hand on the stone at the same time. Taking one last look at the sky, then over her shoulder towards Annabelle and the others, she closed her eyes.

"Here goes," she said to herself, then placed Emilia's and her hands on the stone and hoped.

CHAPTER 14

Emilia.

Emilia's eyes flicked open, it took her a while to process where she was and put it all together. The last thing she could recall was passing out surrounded by wind and a fear that the world was ending. At that moment she was bound tight and could see Ellie who had a look of resolute fear etched all over her face. When Emilia opened her eyes however, she appeared to be resting in Ellie's lap looking up at her. Ellie was looking round, clearly distressed but had not yet noticed that Emilia had woken.

"Did we do it?" Emilia asked in a soft croaky voice. She still did not yet feel like she had her full strength back and even saying that was a significant effort for her.

Ellie looked down sharply but smiled softly, "I don't think so, not really sure what is going on now," she looked up and around once more.

Emilia moved her head slightly and followed her gaze. They were back in the space between spaces, flowing with purple as it always did. This time though it seemed to be behaving differently. The flow of the vapour like colour was more violent than usual and it seemed to be conflicted with itself as to where to go next. Emilia concluded that rather than moving like steam from a cup of tea, it looked more like the rough sea on the shore during the build up to a storm.

"What's going on?" she asked, lifting herself out of Ellie's lap as she did so.

"How much do you remember?" Ellie asked.

Emilia rubbed her head and thought for a moment, "I remember him taking some of my hair, and then my spirit floating up into the sky and creating a huge black hole," she looked at Ellie. "That's it I think, what happened after that?"

Emilia listened as Ellie explained everything she had missed, her emotions catching up with her as she heard certain events. Annabelle being tormented by the Man, her friends trying to get to them but being held back. All of it.

"So, we are back in his realm again?" Emilia asked. "You got us here?"

The girls looked around.

"Something doesn't feel right though, know what I mean?" Emilia added.

"Yes, it feels angry or broken somehow doesn't it?"

The girls looked at each other, worried looks etched over their faces. Before either of them could voice further questions or concerns about their own fate, the fate of their friends, or the world, the silence was broken.

"What did you do? This is not possible," the Man spoke from all around in an angry, frustrated tone.

This comforted the girls, they looked at each other and a small smile crept onto their faces. If he was annoyed, then they had done something positive somewhere.

"Us? We couldn't have done anything, remember?" Emilia said confidently, "You said so yourself that we couldn't beat you."

"You cannot stop me, but you have done something that is causing disruptions in the realm and that has halted the energy flow into my world."

Emilia raised an eyebrow to Ellie, it had worked, at least for now, "That's a shame, just when I was starting to like the big black hole of nothingness," she said confidently.

"How are you here? This should not be possible? Tell me what you have done."

There was more anger in his voice now, he was clearly confused, angry, and very frustrated.

"You first," Ellie chimed in, "You like to talk, so out with it."

Silence. The girls looked at each other and then around the space they were in. Moments later the Man appeared not too far away, facing them. His arms outstretched and his glow back to normal after releasing the need for physical contact once more. They got to their feet to face him.

"What is there for me to tell?" he asked.

"Tell us what all that was, what was that big black hole and why did my spirit help you?" Emilia asked.

"I hid it in the statue the day it was formed. It was set to absorb all the negative energy it could and store it up until the day I released it. That day was today. I released it from its stone prison and activated it with your hair." He turned towards Emilia as he said this, "Doing so caused it to unleash all of the negative energy it had consumed in one go across your planet. It soared into the sky and tore open the gateway between worlds. The black hole you saw is the true connection, the bridge between your world and my own. It will spread, getting wider and covering everything with a darkness so deep that the brightest of lights would not be able to penetrate it. All of the energy from your world would be consumed and passed into my own where it would thrive and wait for me to wield it to create the perfect world."

"You mean the perfect world that you want to exist over ours?" Ellie asked.

"Yes. Once your world had perished the spirits from Imaginari would be free to move into yours and we would create a glorious everlasting planet."

He seemed quite proud of this and himself at this stage, but Emilia had other ideas.

"You really think this would work? Did you really think that destroying our world for the second time, then laying your spirit nonsense over it would work?"

"It will work, it was working."

"Aha," Emilia interrupted. "Was, you said was, so that means it is not working right now?"

There was a moments pause, then he responded sternly, "No it is not, what did you do?"

The girls looked at each other.

"I think you're asking the wrong person," Emilia replied, still looking at Ellie grinning.

"What do you mean? You girls are the only ones that can

possibly be in my way."

Emilia looked at him, "Yes, we are. But we are not the only versions of us involved here tonight, are we?"

She paused, waiting for him to work out what they could possibly have done.

"Impossible," he said finally. Reaching out his left arm and pulling it towards himself as if pulling on a rope. Emilia's spirit appeared and floated slowly towards him. It was glowing with the same brightness it had moments before, clearly it had not finished expelling all the anger and negativity yet. "What did you do?"

The spirit floated in front of him and turned to face the girls, if looked at from above they were now positioned in a triangle with the spirit in its centre.

"We did the same thing you did to me," Ellie stated. "We made a small unnoticeable change," she smiled and looked at Emilia.

"And it appears to have worked," Emilia added, turning back towards the Man.

"Not possible," he exclaimed and reached inside the spirit. Or at least, he tried to. As he reached out a hand clearly expecting to be able to reach inside it, he jerked it away again, as if it had burned him. He tried his other hand, the same thing happened. He moved around the spirit so that he was now between it and the girls, frantically trying to reach inside but each time he flinched away. He looked like a child trying desperately to get at a toy that was just out of reach. After a few failed attempts he turned and glided over to now be between the two girls. They each backed away a little to give him more space.

"Having problems?" Emilia asked pleasantly. She did enjoy being polite when someone was angry.

Facing Emilia, he shouted, "Whatever you have done, it will not work. My power and that of my world is more than you can ever imagine."

"That may be so," Ellie interrupted, the Man turned away from Emilia to look at her. "But have you considered our power and what we can do?"

"What power?" he demanded. "You have no power over me."

"Agreed," Ellie stated. "We do not have power over you, but I have power over the spirit energy now, and most importantly Emilia has power over that spirit," she nodded towards the golden spirit floating a short distance away.

"She has no power over it, it answers to me and only me," he snarled. "I am its true master."

"Are you though?" Emilia asked.

She turned to face the spirit and focused on it. She willed it to her, focusing her energy and strength on it. Nothing happened. After a few painful moments she stopped and took some deep breaths. Glancing at Ellie she could see that she was not overly worried, but Emilia could not understand why.

The Man cackled over them both, "See. There is no power here other than my own. I summoned that spirit here, not you. I control it, not you. Whatever you have done I will find a way to undo it and bring back full control to me and my plan."

"Well, that may not be as easy as you think," Ellie interrupted once again.

The Man turned to her.

"See, you said all along that Emilia was created from me, and that spirit in turn was created from Emilia. So technically, doesn't that mean that spirit is actually part of me?"

Emilia listened, catching her breath as she did so trying to process this as fast as she could.

"Yes, but I claimed it, when it was installed in the stone I gave it the instructions needed, I created the rules."

"Yes, you did," Ellie continued. "But you didn't compensate for us working together, did you?" she nodded at Emilia. "You told it what to do if it felt the touch of one of us, but not us both. You hadn't even contemplated the fact that we may help each other. You are so used to being alone that you have forgotten what it feels like to have help, to have friends."

Emilia looked at her, it was starting to fall into place now.

"So what?" the Man retorted, "I do not need help, I do not need friends."

"That was your biggest mistake, and that is why you will lose tonight. That spirit no longer answers to you because we created a new set of rules. When we both touched the stone, we created a new idea, a new way to do things. Together. We told it that when it felt our combined touch to stop everything and bring us all here." She gestured around, "And here we are. I think that is what is wrong here as well, isn't it? This realm isn't used to having this much power in it and it can't cope."

"Yes, this realm is not designed for it, but it will stand the test as will I."

He turned towards the spirit and started to move towards it. Ellie looked at Emilia, "Do you trust me?" she mouthed silently behind the Man's back.

Emilia nodded.

Ellie smiled warmly and nodded, "It won't work," she said boldly to the Man who was still moving towards the spirit.

He turned to face her, "Why?" he demanded.

"Because I think I am the true owner of that spirit, I can sense it, I can feel it. And I think that means I can control it."

The Man laughed, a bold deep laugh that shook Emilia's stomach the way a firework does when it goes off.

What happened next was a complete blur. The Man started to reply, but before Emilia could process it, she noticed that Ellie had moved, she had made a sweeping movement with her arms. A movement that started at the spirit and ended by pointing at her. Emilia looked round and saw that the golden spirit was flying straight for her. She was about to scream in fear and attempt to leap aside when it collided with her and sent her flying backwards to the floor. She scrambled to her feet and looked all around; the spirit had gone. Emilia felt strong again, life and energy seemingly flowing through her. She looked at Ellie who was beaming at her. Then she turned to the Man who was advancing on her, arms outstretched towards her as if he was going to grab her by the throat.

"Emilia, this may hurt and I'm sorry," she heard Ellie shout.

Before she could process this, she was pulled forwards and moments later released. A feeling of being on a swing that has reached the highest point and then her stomach being left behind as she fell to Earth. Focusing, she saw that the golden spirit had appeared once more and was leaving her body, heading straight towards the Man who was now almost within touching distance of her. She steadied herself, feeling weaker once again, just in time to see it pass through him, his face contorted with pain as it touched him and passed through his ghost like body. Emilia took a small step to the right, bringing Ellie into view. To her amazement, she was making the rope pulling movement that she had seen the Man make to manipulate spirits many times over. Ellie was doing this, she was pulling and pushing that spirit around like it was a yo-yo on a string. As Emilia watched, the Man fell forwards, clearly the contact with the spirit had taken a huge amount of energy from him. She looked at Ellie. Who had now moved her arms and hands into a stopping position, as if she was pushing against a tall heavy object like a wardrobe. She appeared to be absorbing the movement of the spirit into her arms and body whilst keeping the spirit visible in front of her. Just as the Man rose once more and turned to face Ellie, she slammed her hands forwards with all her might forcing the golden spirit away from her. It flew like a cloud flying in the air, away from Ellie and into the Man once more who this time was flattened onto his back as the spirit passed through. Instinctively, Emilia reached out to grab their golden accomplice, the moment that she made contact with it, it vanished once more, and she felt a surge of energy and strength flow through her.

"How are you doing this?" she asked Ellie.

"I'll explain later, but I need that back," came the frantic reply.

Emilia understood and braced for the sensation of having her spirit removed once again. The Man was still down but was starting to rise once again between the two girls. Emilia saw Ellie making the same rope pulling motion and then felt the energy drain out of her almost instantly as the golden spirit appeared. Just as before, it slammed into the Man hitting him on the head first and flipping him over onto his back once more. Emilia could now see Ellie's plan. With each contact with the golden spirit, the Man weakened. Each time she slammed it through him he got weaker, and his glow faded. By contrast, the golden spirit seemed unharmed by the constant push and pull from Ellie. Once more she slammed it back across him and into Emilia's chest. Emilia knew she could not do anything to help, but simply using her body as a wall for Ellie to bounce the spirit off was helping. It was giving Ellie a chance and she was taking it with both hands. After several passes, the Man was no longer lifting himself off the ground. At this point, Ellie stopped clearly exhausted and allowed the golden spirit to float near her as she walked over towards Emilia. The two girls stood over the Man who was on his back looking up at them, clearly weakened, his ghost like glow fading.

"How did you do that?" Emilia asked.

"Magic," Ellie winked between deep breaths, "I took a chance it worked."

They hugged.

"You cannot undo what is done," the Man said quietly from the floor.

"Yes, we can, the same way that we couldn't beat you remember?" Emilia retorted.

"How?"

The girls looked at each other, "Like we have said many times," Ellie said, taking Emilia's hand.

"Together," Emilia finished for her.

"Why are you helping each other? Why are you doing this?"

The girls looked at him and said nothing.

Ellie reached out and beckoned the spirit over to them, it glided over silently. With a small movement of her hands Ellie was able to lift it up and over the Man so it was now floating horizontally above him, lined up with his fading form.

"This is where it ends," Ellie said coldly and lowered her arms.

As she did so the spirit began to move slowly towards the floor, towards the Man that was motionless and unable to move.

"But I made her from the worst of you, why are you both trying to help each other?" he screamed just before the spirit touched him.

Ellie pushed harder, making it move slowly down into him as

he lay on the floor crying out in pain.

"No, you showed me who I needed to be to beat you," Ellie replied.

As she did so, the spirit reached the floor and was now completely covering the Man as he lay there. He let out a howl of pain as Ellie forced the spirit into him, pinning him down. He was fading, the spirit was absorbing him and dissolving his form. As his cries reached an ear-splitting volume he shattered and exploded all around them into wisps of shining sparkles of light. Emilia's spirit lifted itself up and was upright once more looking at the two girls.

Ellie relaxed her arms and exhaled, "Well, that was exciting," she chuckled, and they fell into each other's arms in a deep hug.

"That was incredible," Emilia said as they pulled apart, "You are incredible."

"We are incredible," Ellie corrected with a smirk.

Emilia looked around, "Do you think that's it? Has he gone?"

Ellie mirrored her looks, "Not sure, but I think he is more gone than the last time."

They turned their attention to the floating spirit.

"What do we do with it?" Emilia asked, a puzzled look on her face.

"Well, we need to fix that black hole and send all that energy back, maybe it can do that?"

They looked at each other and shrugged. Emilia took a step back and Ellie closed her eyes and focused on the spirit in her mind. Seconds later the spirit shattered into millions of shards of light and spread out across the purple landscape. As it reached the walls, ceiling, and floor, they immediately calmed and returned to the gentle sway that the girls were used to.

"Wow, how did you do that?" Emilia asked in amazement.

"I just sort of, thought it," Ellie replied as she opened her eyes. "Hard to explain really, do you think it worked?"

"Only one way to find out, we need to get back. How do we do that?"

They looked at each other, they had not considered this. Before either of them could say anything else the golden spirit returned once more, a little fainter this time having expelled and spent its energy fixing everything that had just happened. Or at least that is what they hoped. Ellie looked at it and focused her mind once more, willing it to help them. Emilia watched on in wonder, she was in awe at what Ellie was doing in front of her. Then Ellie's face turned to one of fear and sadness.

Emilia went over and put her arm around her, "What is it?" she asked.

Ellie looked at her, tears forming as she reached out and pulled Emilia into a tight hug. As Emilia hugged back, Ellie muttered between sobs, "It can only do one thing, and we need it to do two," she wept.

Emilia pulled away so she could look at Ellie, "What do you mean, two things?"

Ellie wiped her face and tried to look as calm as possible, "I can feel it, I can sense it. That is how I was able to control it. I don't really understand but I can almost talk to it."

"Ok, keep going," Emilia comforted.

"Because we used so much of the energy to kill him, and then to fix everything, which is done by the way. It can only do one of the two things we need."

"What two things? What are you talking about?" Emilia was confused and wanted to help and understand.

Ellie sobbed some more, "I want it to take us home, take us out of here."

"That's one, what is the other?"

Ellie looked at Emilia with wide eyes and Emilia knew without anything else being said.

"The other is that I want it to keep you alive," Ellie muttered between sobs.

The two girls looked at each other in silence for a few moments, lit by the golden glow from the spirit that was floating near them.

"Well, there is only one option isn't there?" Emilia stated, fighting back the tears.

Ellie looked at her.

"You need to tell it to take you home, it has always been yours. I am just a creation to try and end everything." She could no longer hold back the tears now; emotion was fully taking over Emilia as she was standing there, "Simon, Leo, Dan, Tyler, Mum, and Dad," she sniffed, "Annabelle. They are all yours and will always belong to you, you need to go and be with them."

Ellie was in floods of tears now, "But I couldn't have done this without you," she sobbed.

"Yes, you could," Emilia comforted. "Remember, I am you. A split-out part of you but you all the same. Ellie, you need to finish this, you did finish this. You beat him, not me."

Ellie grabbed Emilia and pulled her into a tight hug, "You know that's not true."

Emilia hugged back, "Yes it is. And you know that there is only one choice here."

Emilia knew it was the only way, there was no point in her staying alive if it meant they had to stay here in this space between spaces. She took Ellie by the shoulders and looked into her eyes, "Look at me." Ellie did so. "You know it is the only way, what is the point in us both staying here, you need to go. You did what you needed to do to save us, all of us. This is what I need to do. Let me do it."

The girls locked eyes, and for a moment just looked at each other. There was an understanding between them, a knowledge that they were stuck. The Man may have gone but he was still having the last laugh. Emilia let go and stood up to her full height.

"Now, I want this to be on my terms, so, what happens next?" she wiped tears away.

Ellie too stood and looked Emilia in the eye, "Well, I can get it to absorb the last parts of your energy, that will give it a final boost that will allow it to get me back home. When I pass through it will move back into me and I will have my full spirit back," she covered her face to hide the tears at the end of this.

"It's ok," Emilia said, holding back tears herself. "This is the way it has to be, and I am willing to do this, just promise me one thing?"

Ellie looked at her.

"Don't forget me, don't forget what we did here together."

Ellie nodded, "I won't. I promise."

Ellie looked at the spirit and waved a hand in Emilia's direction. It slowly moved towards her as it made contact, she felt a surge of energy once more. Ellie faced her and gave her one last smile, "I'm sorry," she said softly.

"Don't be, it's ok."

Ellie made another pulling motion and Emilia felt the energy drain out of her. With her last thoughts she decided to say one last thing, "Ellie, look after Annabelle. We love her, let her know that we love her."

That was all she could manage. With one last look at Ellie, she closed her eyes and drifted. To Emilia it felt like going to sleep, a deep sleep that would keep her safe and warm in the knowledge that she had done what she needed to do. Ellie on the other hand had just watched Emilia fade into dust. She collapsed to her knees and sobbed uncontrollably, with nothing but the glow of her golden spirit to keep her company surrounded by purple vapour. The only noise was the sound of her own tears and sobs, as she wailed in pain for the loss, the loss of a friend that she did not even know she had.

CHAPTER 15

Ellie could not move, she was stricken by grief and could not lift herself off the floor, she did not know what to do. Even though it appeared she had succeeded in defeating the Man, she felt like she had lost. His promise of the world falling apart around her suddenly felt very real. Looking round with nothing but a floating spirit that looked like Emilia for company, in a space surrounded by purple vapour was not the best place for her to deal with her pain. She sat and crossed her legs, picking at her fingers in frustration and disappointment, sobbing. She intended to stay there until she was not crying anymore and only then would she return to her friends. But would they be her friends? Was she going back to a time when Emilia was the known person, meaning that her family would ask where their daughter was? What would Ellie do? Where would she go? Had her world ended? These were all questions that were going around in her head and were not helping with her need to stop crying. She looked up at the spirit, it was floating a short distance away gently bobbing up and down.

"Did you know this would happen?" Ellie asked, not really expecting a reply.

"There is always sacrifice," came a soft voice, not from the direction Ellie expected though. It came from all around.

Ellie got to her feet and looked around, "Who's there?" she demanded.

"We wanted to come and see for ourselves; we felt the change in the flow and wanted to come and see you again."

"Guardians?" Ellie asked, not really sure of herself.

"Yes, we have not been able to venture here for a very long

time, he kept us at bay but now he has gone we are able once more to travel between worlds."

"So, you can go home?"

"We can, but we will continue to stay in your world and move between them."

Ellie was confused by this; she could not help but think that going home would have been the first thing they wanted to do. "Why don't you want to go home? To stay in your world?"

"Balance," came the simplistic reply. "We have come to understand the balance between our worlds. We believe that one cannot survive without the other, they are linked in a circle of energy."

"I have had this explained to me before, you need the energy from our world to sustain yours, but what do we get from yours that makes it a circle?" Ellie asked confused.

"Your world exists because of the energy that it gets from the Sun, light and heat create this energy and it is used by everything that is living. The energy that we use in our world is used in a way that allows us to cycle it back to you, we borrow it. When we have used it, it is passed back into your world once again. If we did not do this, your world would suffer under the burden of too much energy, life would become saturated with it and it would perish."

"Like how we can die from drinking too much water?" Ellie tried to rationalise and understand what she was being told.

"Yes, your world needs this energy, but if it was left to build up it would cause it to suffer. We believe we need to stay to maintain the balance as much as we can."

"You're going to stay, hidden in our clouds?"

"We will continue to move between worlds but yes, we have found that moving through your skies as vapour allows us to absorb the energy and filter it back down to your world. Now that the Man is out of the way, and we can operate freely, this will be much easier for us to do all over your planet."

"Is he really gone?" Ellie asked, looking at the spirit as she did so.

"His form has dissolved, and his power and control has released this realm. As such we believe he has gone, yes."

Ellie breathed a deep sigh of relief.

"Know this though, nothing is ever truly lost. Energy is never lost; it is always maintained in a balance and as such is never gone for good."

This unnerved Ellie, "So you mean he may be back?"

"He might, but he might not. You used that spirit well to dissolve him and he will have been spread far and wide, it is possible he will never be able to regain his form and terrorise you, your world, or Imaginari."

"What about Emilia?" Ellie asked, a lump forming in her throat as she said her name. "Is she gone too?"

"She is."

Ellie's head dropped, tears forming once more.

"However, she was made from you, that spirit you see before you is hers, but it came from you. She was always a part of you and that will never change."

"Energy is only borrowed," Ellie said defiantly as she lifted her head once more to look at the spirit.

"Correct. That which is borrowed must be returned. She will live in your memory as much as you want her to, it is true that the Man made her to aid his plans, but you used that against him and that was his ultimate downfall."

Ellie smiled, "Emilia would have liked that, knowing that she got the last word. She would have wanted that."

"Yes, but now it is time for you to go, there is more to discuss but that can wait."

"More?" Ellie asked. "What more do you want from me?"

"We want nothing from you, we want to share knowledge with you, we want to help you understand as much as possible. But now, we want you to mourn, and be with your friends."

"Are they my friends?"

"They are, and always will be."

Ellie smiled and looked at the golden spirit once more, "What will happen to it?"

"As you pass through it to get home it will attach itself to you and once again you will be whole. Everything the Man did has been undone, so this spirit is yours once more."

It glowed and seemed to agree with this statement from the ghost like voice around them. Ellie took steps towards it, as she did so it moulded itself to fit her body perfectly. She made contact and moved into it, closing her eyes as she did so to shield them from the golden light. Ellie felt a warmth spread through her, no pain just a comforting feeling that covered her entire body. She took a deep breath and one final step, as her foot was lowered to the floor it seemed to miss and keep going. Before Ellie knew what was happening she was falling forwards and landing face first in a heap on the damp grass.

Ellie did not need to look around to know where she was. The grass was firm, the sky was dark, and she could hear and feel the sound of pounding feet heading towards her. She sat up and looked around, she was back by the Statue Of Mow on her knees. Around her the grass was normal, as were the trees and bushes, the sky had returned to its normal deep blue colour and the swirling clouds around the giant black hole had gone. The feet she was aware of belonged to her friends; it was no surprise to Ellie that they were being led by Annabelle. Ellie stood and turned to face them moments before they got to her. Annabelle clattered into her and wrapped her in a hug pushing her to the floor once again. Moments later, Ellie was surrounded by all of them firing questions at her.

"What happened?" Leo shouted.

"Are you ok?" Dan wanted to know.

"Is he gone?" Simon chimed in.

"We tried to help you, but we couldn't get close," Annabelle stated shamefully.

Ellie looked at her, "Why say it like that? It wasn't your fault."

"I know but, I don't want you to be alone. I'm meant to help you, I'm on your team," Annabelle blushed a shade of pink.

Ellie smiled, "It's fine, I know you are."

"Stop flirting you two and tell us what happened," Simon shouted.

"Ok," Ellie grinned looking at him. "What happened here first, how long have we been gone?"

"Which time? You went in there not long after we found you on the hill over there," Simon pointed behind him. "Then you came back, and we got to see him for the first time, he floated up above the rocks and made a huge black hole that was sucking the colour out of everything."

Then Annabelle took over, "Then you went back in again, it got really bad out here for a moment then not long after it just stopped."

"Yeah," Leo added. "The black sky, the clouds, all of it just sort of stopped and went back to normal. Then about a minute later you appeared here and now we are here talking to you."

All four looked at her expectantly.

Ellie processed this, but something did not feel right to her, "You said you found me over there?" she asked, looking at Simon.

"Yeah, you stormed away from us up the hill, we decided to leave you to it and went back to Annabelle's for a bit. Then the sky started to turn black, so we came up here to find you and see what was going on. That's when we found you over there in a heap. We started to call an ambulance, but you came too just after, so we stopped them. Then you went in, wherever you went, and you know the rest."

Ellie blinked, "I stormed away from you?"

"Yes, we were having drinks at the pub and you got upset and left us. We tried to call you, but you weren't answering so we thought it best to leave you alone for a bit."

"Why did I leave?" Ellie was very confused now, she looked at Annabelle for comfort.

Annabelle looked down and muttered, "Because we fell out, about something silly that doesn't matter." She looked up at Ellie, and seeing her face decided to say more, "I was acting jealously, and it was silly, and I'm sorry. I promise it doesn't matter now."

"You were acting jealous?" Ellie stated, confusion was all she was feeling now.

"Yes, I'm sorry, can we please not fight again?" she took Ellie's hand, "Please?"

Ellie smiled, "I don't want to fight, I want to understand. I want to understand what happened here and what is going on."

They looked at her, "What do you mean?" Annabelle asked. "Surely you know more than we do Ellie?"

Ellie looked at them, "Ok, I left you all, then you all went to Annabelle's?"

They nodded.

"What did you do there?"

"We chatted, ate some food then when the clouds changed up here, we came to look for you." Simon replied.

"And when you got here, I was over there, passed out?"

They nodded again.

"Nobody near me? How did I wake up?"

"Nobody was up here apart from you, you came round on your own, we couldn't do anything to help."

Ellie stood, a look of alarm on her face, and turned to face the Statue Of Mow, "What did you do?" she asked quietly.

The others stood around her, "Ellie, tell us what happened," Annabelle said calmly, taking Ellie's hand as she did so. "Let us in."

Ellie leant on Annabelle's shoulder, "What you are all telling me is not what I have experienced in the last day or so. It is completely different, and I don't even know where to begin."

She paused, trying to work out what to say and do next, there was so much to tell. Emilia, being welcomed back by them all, learning to control the spirit energy, the Man, time travel, and the bit that hurt the most, Emilia dissolving in front of her. She shivered, "Can we walk and talk? It's cold up here."

Annabelle squeezed her hand, "Whatever you need."

The group turned away from the statue and started to walk away, Ellie in the middle of her friends. She was almost certain that they were completely her friends again. They headed off the grass and onto the road, Ellie starting to tell her story as they walked.

"I will tell you what I know then you guys help me filling in the blanks, ok?"

They all agreed.

"It all started a couple of days ago, when I was planning on coming to surprise Annabelle."

"You did surprise me, we went for a drink and you bought that picture of the statue and all sorts."

"See, for me, that didn't happen."

They all stopped and looked at her.

"Let me explain. I went to the statue and got pulled into it, whilst I was in there the Man, he did something, he made a copy of me is the only way I can word it. When I made it back here and fell out of the statue again Emilia was there, Emilia Fields. She was me. And for me it was her that met you for a drink and that got angry with you all."

They kept walking, the group listening to everything Ellie said, Ellie felt comforted by this but recalling everything that had happened was not the easiest thing for her to do.

"For me, Emilia was the one that argued with you all and left for the hill. Then at Annabelle's we talked, but none of you knew who I was, you had all forgotten me as if I had never existed. Then when we saw the sky start to change, I left for home, then we met up here on the hill."

"You're saying that we forgot you?" Simon asked, curiously.

"Yes. When we got here Emilia was the one who was knocked out and I revived her."

"How?" Annabelle asked, "How did you do that?"

Ellie stopped; this was the bit she was most worried about. "I used the energy flow, the spirit energy that all this is about. I can use it now and control it I think, I pulled energy into her and revived her enough to help us move her."

They were all looking at her now.

"Then we, Emilia and I, made it back into the statue. We travelled in time and laid a trap for the Man, when you say I reappeared around the time the sky went black. For me it was an us, Emilia was right there with me. He used her spirit to rip open the sky and start pulling all of the energy into Imaginari."

"You travelled in time?" Leo asked a suspicious look on his face.

"I know how it sounds but I promise its true," Ellie pleaded, moving forwards to carry on walking. "We were able to turn that spirit against him, I was able to control it and manipulate it, we used it to destroy him and reset everything he had done. Apparently, this also reset everything meaning you had no idea she ever existed."

"If she was made from you," Annabelle commented, "Did she ever really exist?"

This struck a chord with Ellie and a tear formed at the corner of her eye. "She did to me," she said softly. "To me she was a part of me that helped, and it kills me that I couldn't save her."
They walked the rest of the journey in silence, Ellie wiping the tears from her face as they did so.

After a short while they had made it home, to Ellie it seemed to take an age. The house was dark, it was the middle of the night and they stopped at the top of the driveway.
"Can we all sneak in?" Leo asked.
Ellie smiled, "Yes just be really quiet."
Not long after they had made it to Ellie's bedroom and to her relief it was back as she remembered it. Crucially for Ellie, all the pictures had been restored to show her with her family and friends. She picked up the one on the bedside table, it was of her and Annabelle. Most importantly, this was the one that had first alerted her to the problem of Emilia. She turned to face the group; they were all sat expectantly around the room.
"The most important thing I want to talk about is how I can manipulate the energy flow; I can use it. That is how we beat him. When I left Annabelle's, I came here."
"Why here? Where were we?" Dan asked.
"You were still at Annabelle's; we had agreed to meet on the hill. I came here because this is where I was in the dream I had, the dream that first showed me I could control the spirit energy. I came here and practiced by the stone in the garden, I ended up meeting a group of spirits that called themselves the Guardians." There were a few raised eyebrows at this. "They are the same as the Man, they tried to stop him before." Ellie continued, explaining how the Man had supposedly wiped out the dinosaurs when the Guardians stood against him. She went over how she and Emilia had gone back in time and changed the rules of the spirit, so they could use it. Her friends listened intently, offering words of encouragement and support. The most interesting question came up when she had reached the point in the story where she was able to control Emilia's spirit, using it to weaken the

Man and eventually destroy him.

"What does that feel like?" Leo asked, an innocent look on his face.

"What?"

"When you control and manipulate it, the spirit energy stuff, how does that feel?"

Ellie paused, she had not really considered it like that, "Strange," was the first word she uttered, much to the amusement of her friends. "The first time it felt like the energy was manipulating me; I wasn't really controlling it if that makes sense? It felt like warm water flowing over me, through me even. When I got to the hill with you all that's when I tried to focus on it for the first time."

"What happened?"

Ellie explained how she had revived Emilia using the energy, and then how they had gone into the statue to face him once more. This was reaching the most painful parts of the story for Ellie now.

"You were both there? In that purple realm thing?" Simon asked.

Ellie nodded, a lump in her throat. "We knew we had done something right because he was so agitated, angry even. As we were talking to him, I began to sense that spirit, I could feel it each time it moved as if it was drawn to me or something. I decided to take a risk and focused on it. I pushed it into Emilia first, as a way of testing if I could do it but also knowing doing so would give Emilia a burst of energy. From then, I knew I could do it. I pulled it out of her and slammed it around through the Man over and over, back and forth like a yo-yo. It was exhausting but adrenaline got me through. Eventually he ended up on his back, fading and unable to move so I positioned it above him and forced it down onto him. This scattered him, and he vanished, dissolved like sugar in water."

Ellie looked at Annabelle, tears forming in her eyes as she did so.

"Then what happened?" Annabelle asked.

"Then I made that spirit undo everything that he had done, I made it expel all of the energy it had stored up to fix everything. What I didn't know was that doing that meant that it would not be able to keep Emilia alive too. It could only save both of us if we stayed in that realm. So, Emilia, told me to-" she stopped, tears and emotions taking over.

Annabelle stepped forward and wrapped Ellie in a hug, "She told you to save yourself, didn't she?"

Ellie nodded, sniffing as she did so, "She told me that it was the only thing to do, that us both living but unable to come back was silly. I promise I tried everything to save her, I really did, but there was nothing I could do."

"I know, we know," Annabelle comforted. She held Ellie tight, trying to comfort and protect her as best she could.

"The last thing she said to me, was something I already knew but hearing it from her made it even more real. Knowing that she was me and I her, meant I was hearing it from myself."

Annabelle pulled away, "What did she say?"

Ellie looked at Annabelle's beautiful round face, "That I love you."

Silence fell over the room; Ellie was immediately aware that this was the first time she had said that to Annabelle, and it was in front of all their friends. Male friends at that and could sense they were all trying to look away and appear not interested whilst holding back small smirks.

To Ellie's delight and surprise, Annabelle smiled, "I love you too, Ellie. I love you too." They smiled at each other and then smirked themselves, "Ok boys, time to go I think. We can catch up on this more later," Annabelle ordered.

The boy's muttered noises of frustration but eventually agreed to leave, Annabelle saw them out making sure they did not disturb Nicholas or Katherine, leaving Ellie to have a quick shower and get sorted for bed. When they were both ready, Ellie in bed and Annabelle on the camp bed on the floor, they turned out the light.

"I did mean it you know; I do love you," Ellie said to the darkness.

"I know, and I do too," Annabelle replied.

Ellie smiled to herself, everything was back as it was, and, in some ways, it was better than it was before. She had never truly expressed her feelings properly to Annabelle, but the courage shown by Emilia had opened that particular way of thinking to her.

The next few days passed without incident, which Ellie was very grateful for. Before she knew it, it was the weekend again and she was walking with Annabelle over the hill in the middle of the village. They soon wandered around the hilltop and were heading towards the Statue Of Mow. They paused when they reached it and looked up at the stone, Ellie was thankful that there was no humming or vibration this time. They stood at the fence which had since been repaired, Annabelle leaning on Ellie's shoulder, enjoying the clear blue sky and summer sun.

"Do you think he will be back?" Annabelle asked.

They had discussed the events at length over the last few days, and this was the one thing that Ellie could not answer fully.

"I hope not," she offered weakly. "Not sure I can handle being caught out again."

"Why not be ready next time then?" Annabelle asked.

"Sounds like you want there to be a next time," Ellie commented, mock surprise in her voice.

"No, but if you were ready. Able to take him on, may be different is all. You told us yourself that when you took him on head to head you beat him easily."

"The spirit beat him easily," Ellie corrected, "I didn't do that much."

"You controlled it, you told it what to do, that's awesome," Annabelle replied, kissing Ellie on the cheek as she did so.

Ellie smiled, "Maybe, who knows. I'd rather he didn't come back though."

"Well, if he does, we will be ready whatever happens."

The girls smiled at each other and turned to head away from the rocks, back towards the Fields family home.

CHAPTER 16

Ellie's summer returned to normal, a mix of work, time out with friends, especially Annabelle, and spending time with family. Everything that she wanted it to be at the beginning. Her relationship with Annabelle was on a sure footing and the two were very happy together, much to the delight of their friends and family. The only thing that was bugging Ellie was the fate of Emilia. Even though she knew that what had happened could not have gone any other way, she felt like there was more she could have done. She would often keep herself awake at night playing back the events over and over in her mind looking for something that she had missed. Annabelle had initially tried to talk her round on this, trying to convince Ellie that she should relax and stop punishing herself, but it was no use so even she had given up with that conversation. Ellie knew she was only trying to help, so had not allowed it to turn into an argument between them. In fact the girls had not really argued again that summer. On this particular day Ellie was reminded of the events that had changed her view of the world she lived in once more, and more specifically the world that ours was connected to, Imaginari. It had been just twenty-four hours between meeting Emilia on the hill and then defeating the Man and finding out she had been removed from all memory. That short time seemed like an eternity when Ellie was living it though. Ellie was reminded of the events as she was sat in her bedroom looking out of the window after doing her jobs at home. Annabelle was at work and they were meeting up later, she had time to kill. With a wry smile Ellie decided to go for a walk up to the folly and to the Statue Of Mow. She did not know why, she did not know if it was a good idea either, but she did know it was something she wanted to do. Packing a small bag with some water and some snacks, Ellie then headed up the hill once again. No matter what happened, this would always be a wonderful place to walk and clear her head. It did not take long for her to reach the folly and to take in the views. Over the past week or so she had overheard people talking all about the freak storm that appeared and disappeared over the hill, nothing like the attention from a few years ago but it was there. Whenever Ellie heard anything like this she would simply smile and keep her head down, she did not need or want any extra attention for that. Ellie stood and watched as the world passed her by, taking in deep cleansing breaths as she did so allowing her body to relax. Ever since she had become aware of her ability to sense the energy around her and what it really meant and did, she had found a new appreciation for the world. As strange as it was, everything seemed brighter and cleaner to Ellie. She smiled to herself, happy in the knowledge that all was well. Looking around, she saw families having picnics on the hill, children playing, and dogs running with an innocence that she knew she would never have again, but that was ok, Ellie knew she had something much better.

After a while, Ellie decided to move onto the Statue Of Mow, just like she did before she walked passed the folly, down the crest of the hill, and along the path. It was quieter here, the focal point for visitors was always the folly and these paths were only really used by locals and farmers. It did not take her long to get there, and she did not see anyone else the whole time that she was walking. Once Ellie reached the pile of rocks and the fence surrounding them she stopped to admire them. Just like the folly this had a different meaning to her now, the experience had been a short but intense one and she would never forget the first time that she was able to feel the energy around her. The stones stood proud above her, the blue sky shaping them perfectly with the sun lighting every little crack and nook hidden by the stone. Ellie felt a sense of relief and perhaps more surprisingly, a sense of purpose. She knew that her ability to sense the energy around her was a side effect of something terrible, but she was also beginning to believe in everything happening for a reason. She kept looking at the stones, reminding herself that it was here she had started to hear a humming sound that had lured her to the rocks before. To her delight, there was no humming or buzzing, indeed the only sound that she was aware of was that of the trees rustling in the wind. Ellie was however aware of a tingle at her fingertips. She was leaning on the fence with her arms crossed under her chin, and the tips of the fingers on her right hand were near the top of some weeds that were growing up the fence post. At first Ellie thought nothing of it as she assumed that it was simply the feeling of being tickled by the plants as they moved in the wind. She shifted slightly to move her hand away from that post and the tingle stopped almost immediately. Ellie could no longer ignore it though, she was fascinated to know and understand what it was, so she unfolded her arms and intentionally moved her hand towards the post once again. As it got closer, the tingle returned. She turned and knelt, keen to conduct an experiment and see what would happen. She reached her palm down to the ground towards the long grass. To her amazement, the tingle returned, she lowered her palm closer still. It never increased to more than a tingle, and she probably would not have noticed if she was not now looking for it after feeling it by mistake on the weeds by the fence post. Ellie put her other hand down, the same feeling reached through her fingertips and palms, a warm tingle that seemingly spread through her wrist and up into the lower part of her arm.

"Amazing," she said out loud.

Ellie sat on the floor, it was comfier than kneeling, and pushed her hands right into the long grass. The feeling was sensational, to Ellie it was like lowering your hands into a warm bath to pull the plug out. The feeling of warmth spread through her hands and wrists up into her arms, Ellie could not see anything, but she knew what it was.

"The energy," she confirmed to herself, again out loud.

Ellie looked around, making sure there was nobody near.

There was not, so she decided to be brave. Ellie closed her eyes and pushed hard into the ground and focused on the energy. She imagined it flowing from the ground into her hands in the same way water from a tap flows into a bowl. After a few moments the feeling of warmth grew stronger, it had reached her upper arms now and was seeping into her chest. With every breath Ellie could feel herself becoming more energetic, the way that she would feel after going for a run. Energised. Eyes still closed, she grinned as her body was now filled with the warmth of the energy flowing through her, into her. She opened her eyes and lifted her hands to look at them. They were clean, not a mark on them and not even a glow, but the feeling of energy in her was just as strong. She stood and checked her arms; they too were clean and showed no marks or anything. Then Ellie noticed the ground, the grass around where her hands had been was still green, but it was a duller green than that of those blades around it. It was as if they had been painted more recently and as such were brighter and bolder than those that had been by her hands.

Whatever is borrowed, must be returned, the words echoed in her head like a bell, as if they had not meant anything until this moment. She looked at her hands, then to the ground and back again.

"So, I can use this, but if I don't give it back then wherever the energy came from will suffer?" Ellie asked herself, "Makes sense I suppose," she mused.

Ellie lowered her arms and as she did so the question, how do I put it back? crossed her mind. Within seconds, she became aware of the warmth flowing out of her hands in the same way it had come in, flowing back into the ground. It felt the same as before only the other way around, and although Ellie could not see it happening, she could see the colour and strength of the grass returning in line with the level of warmth flowing out of her. First her chest returned to normal, then her arms and finally her hands and fingers. As the last drop moved out of her back to the ground the final blades of grass returned to a bold green.

"Amazing," she shouted, bouncing up and down with glee and uncontrollable excitement. Immediately, Ellie wanted to try something else, something bigger. She hurried over to a nearby tree, for a moment she thought it may have been the one that she had hidden behind with Emilia, then she focused on the feeling of the energy once more and within seconds it had started again. Stronger this time, it moved much faster through her body and before long she stopped and focused on the tree. Unlike the grass, it seemed to show no sign of decay at this point, so Ellie moved away slowly, sensing her body as she did so. It was unlike anything she had experienced before; it was as if her entire body had been tuned up and made stronger. Her senses seemed more alert, colours were bolder, sounds were crisper. Every breath felt like pure oxygen, her body felt as though it was not working as hard but was performing so much better. Ellie looked around, mainly in awe of the energy she now felt but also to check she was still alone. She was. Her eyes fell on a bush that was looking very dry, presumably from the warm weather that had been around the last couple of days. Ellie decided to try something and moved over to it. It came more naturally this time, all she had to do was imagine the energy moving from her into this bush. Within moments it had sprouted new leaves and was no longer brown or looking sorry for itself. It bloomed right in front of Ellie's eyes as the power left her body. When she felt it had been fully restored, there appeared to be some energy left in Ellie. She returned to the tree and put it back. Ellie beamed. She had no idea how she should be able to use this ability, or even if she wanted to, but she did know that she could not wait to show Annabelle. She put out her arms and was now fully aware of everything that was living and moving around her. She turned slowly on the spot sensing the movement through her fingertips as different plants and trees came closer or moved further away from her fingers. She closed her eyes and beamed, then as a final flourish decided to jump and turn as she did so, sensing all the movement and flow around her like leaping through a pile of leaves. She landed and opened her eyes, her surroundings had gone, she was once again surrounded by purple smoke and vapour.

Ellie's smile faded, the euphoria she had just been feeling disappeared very quickly as she stood and took in where she was once more.

"Welcome, Eleanor," came a soft voice, but not one that she had heard before.

Ellie turned, and as she did so, found herself surrounded by four spirits, identical to that of the Man standing in a circle around her.

"I'm hoping you are who I think you are," Ellie stated calmly, determined not to lose her cool.

"We are the four Guardians, yes," came the soft reply.

Ellie turned, trying to work out which of them had spoken, "Can you move a little? This is going to make me dizzy trying to work out who is talking."

Within seconds the four spirits had whirled round her and were now standing in a line in front of her.

"Thank you," she said, a little intimidated by the speed and movement.

"We mean you no harm, we talk as one, so you need not worry which of us to look at."

Ellie nodded, "Ok, so, what's up?" she had relaxed a lot now, having previously decided to trust these spirits until she had a reason not to.

"We wanted to have a conversation about what has happened and what happens next," came the reply.

"Didn't we already do that? You helped me by the stone and then arrived just in time to watch me destroy Emilia?"

Her voice cracked a little at the end of that, she did not blame them for this, but they were the closest thing she could blame.

"Yes, we did. But now we want to share the full picture with you, give you all the information we have so that you can be as prepared as possible for what may, or may not, happen in the future."

Ellie sighed, "So, you mean this isn't over?"

"We mean it might not be."

"Ok, I'm listening."

"Good. As you know this is not the first time that he has

had to be stopped. Indeed, you yourself have stopped him twice. The first time was millions of years ago, when we first discovered your world. We too thought as he did; that we could use more of the energy in one go to change Imaginari for the better. We came, and we explored."

As Ellie listened, the purple vapour dissolved revealing a lush rainforest, squawking birds, roaring animals, and dense trees and foliage.

"Is this real?" Ellie asked, nervously, she was finding it difficult to tell the difference between recreations and real life at this point.

"No, this is a recreation so that we can show you and explain."

Ellie relaxed a little.

"We want to show you what we wanted to do," they continued. "This is your world about sixty-five million years ago; it was a lush and prosperous planet. The creatures here were primitive but they understood the balance of life and death. Without knowing it they understood more about the flow of energy from your world into ours than humans ever have."

"What do you mean? Surely we are more intelligent than dinosaurs?"

"We did not say more intelligent, we said they understood more. You see, they existed for one reason, survival. They did what they needed to do in order to live. The same can be said for animals that still exist in your world today, they do what they need to do to survive. Humans behave differently however. Humans want to progress, push boundaries, and explore. In doing so they can hurt the worlds balance, it is a delicate balance that must be kept in check."

They had moved above the trees now, Ellie was beginning to feel a little sick as she felt like she was viewing footage of a jungle from a drone, but in virtual reality complete with smells and wind.

"Where are we going?" she asked.

"We are going to the breach point between worlds, the portal if you will."

They carried on climbing until eventually the ground

stopped getting smaller beneath them.

"Here, it is at this point we want to show you."

Seconds later, the clouds froze, and everything stopped still.

"This is the point where the most energy flows between worlds. What you are about to see is an enhanced view of what happens, but it is invisible to us and you. We believe you will be able to sense it the same way we do though."

The clouds separated, and a large hole appeared in the sky. Being this high up, Ellie had no point of reference but felt it looked like the size of a football stadium. The hole was black, the same as the one the Man had created above the statue to try and destroy life on Earth.

"Energy moves from your world to ours," they added, as they did so familiar strands of golden yellow light moved from the ground into the hole. They started off small and grouped together through the sky as they got nearer to the hole, the moment they hit it they disappeared. "The portal will pull the energy from your world and push it together, then in our world it beams down onto the surface sending the energy pulsating through everything and everyone. That energy is used by us, it sustains us and allows us to exist. We have a limited life span though, and once we have served our purpose and our time is up, our bodies dissolve and are pulled back through the same portals into your world once more."

As if to demonstrate this, blue shafts of light appeared in the middle of the portal, but rather than flowing back down to the ground, they dissolved very quickly into blue particles, forming mists and clouds in the sky. These clouds got bigger, still with a haze of blue until they were so big and black that they turned to rain clouds and poured down over the ground below.

"You see, the energy that comes back into your world creates life, it eventually turns into water which is then turned into life and sustains more energy in your world that then comes into Imaginari. This is the Cycle of Existence."

"Cycle of Existence," Ellie repeated taking it all in.

"Yes, this is the balance and the cycle that sustains life in our world and creates life in yours. It is, now more than ever, at risk though."

"How?" Ellie asked intrigued, this was sounding more like a science lesson than a warning from spirits right now.

"First, let us explain what happened here, and what he has tried to do twice again since."

The scene changed once more, the black hole was still there with the energy flows coming and going, but it was now surrounded by five spirits. Ellie assumed that these were the four she was with now and the Man.

"We were all in agreement, we used our energy to force the to portal open wider and pull in more energy in one go. We all believed it would allow our world to thrive and that yours would be able to survive."

The golden yellow strands grew bolder and brighter. They were getting wider as they got closer to the ground. As they watched, Ellie could see the areas nearest to the larger strands perishing, entire areas of trees and plants were turning from lush green to brown. Animals were dying and seemingly decaying in seconds instead of months or years.

"We soon realised that doing this would not work, that removing too much in one go would destroy your world and then eventually ours, so we tried to put an end to it."

Ellie looked at the five spirits in the recreation, they had all moved away from the hole now; all except one. To Ellie's surprise, the group of four lashed out beams of green, like a cowboy with a lasso. Each of the four strands wrapped around a different part of the remaining figure, that Ellie had now worked out to be the Man. They were trying to pull him away, they were all pulling against him, but he was resisting.

"This is the moment we failed," came a solemn comment from the spirits she was with.

After a few moments, the Man seemed to lurch forward, jerking all four of the other spirits towards him and the portal. The four collided with the one and what happened next was a blur. Ellie saw the man get pushed right into a golden beam of light and get sucked into the portal, presumably to Imaginari. The four spirits also got tangled, but they were entwined with some of the blue energy flowing back to Earth. They were immediately dissolved and seemingly turned to vapour and clouds along with all the other energy flowing into the sky. Moments after that, there was an almighty bang, and a huge surge of power shot out of the middle of the portal towards the ground in the form of a lightning bolt. The moment it hit the Earth, the sky turned black, and Ellie was immediately reminded of the view on the hill once the Man had released the spirit of Emilia from the rock. The sky churned, the ground shook and cracked, spewing hot lava from beneath the earth onto the surface. Looking at the sky, it had now turned into a storm, raining down hail stones. This mixed with the hot steaming floor covered the world with a cloud of ash, smoke, and steam in seconds. Soon all Ellie could see was clouds.

"We failed to stop him, and in our haste to try we also disrupted the flow. What you saw was the fallout of our mistake. He got pulled into our world, but his direct contact with the golden flow sent some of the energy back where it had come from. That is what created the lightning and the lava you just saw. Whereas we got caught in the blue flow and were dispersed into vapour and clouds. Our significant energy there, where it is only supposed to be mild energy returning to your world, created extreme storms, clouds of darkness, and the combination of those two things destroyed most life on your world."

"It was an accident though, you didn't mean it, you tried to stop it," Ellie tried to offer as consolation.

"Correct, but we acted in the wrong way. This proved to us that we must protect the balance of energy and not try to manipulate it for our gain. Doing so would destroy both worlds."

"Ok, I'm with you so far," Ellie stated. "Then he tried again, twice with me, and I know why he waited, that's because he was trying to get back through into my world, right?"

"Correct. He needed time to get his form restored, whilst we were stuck here moving from vapour to vapour, cloud to cloud in the sky above your world he was working to restore his form, so he could try again. He did not believe that there was another way, he wanted to destroy your world to protect ours. We could not stop him because he was able to restore his power before we could restore ours, once he got through, he was able to keep us at bay."

"Where do we come in?" Ellie asked. She wanted to understand what they meant by humans being less knowledgeable than dinosaurs.

"Imagine for a moment that we had not interfered and led to the extinction of the dinosaurs, imagine that life had been allowed to progress the way it had wanted to. The balance would have been maintained. We are here to ensure that balance continues, we owe your world that much."

"What does this have to do with me?" Ellie asked, this seemed to be getting a little deep for her now.

"We believe we will need you, and you will need us. We believe that we will need to work as a team for our worlds to survive."

"Hmmmmmm. How's that then?" Ellie asked a little more sarcastically than she had intended.

"We cannot stop him, he is too strong for us, and if he does return, he will be stronger than ever. You have already stopped him twice and now you seem to have gained the ability to see, manipulate, and most importantly use the energy flow in the way we used to be able to. In short Eleanor, you have the best shot at being the true Guardian of Imaginari."

Ellie was stunned at this, "Me? A Guardian?"

"Yes. You have the physicality and strength from your world, with the ability to use the spirit energy of ours. Therefore, you were able to beat him this time, because he accidentally gave you exactly what he should not have."

"So, this means he will be back?"

"As we said, we believe he is gone but if we prepare as if he is not then you will be ready. We will be ready, and together we can beat him for good."

The clouds had gone now, and they were back in the realm of purple vapour.

"How can I be ready? What can I do?"

"Practice. You have already manipulated a tree and a bush have you not? Try over and over, remember to restore the energy when you are done. See what you can do, push

boundaries, be the inquisitive human we know you to be."
"You mean you want me to get ready to fight?"
"We want you to be the person you were born to be. Be the fifth Guardian."

As they finished this last sentence, the purple vapour dissolved, and Ellie was back on the hilltop exactly where she was with the trees and bushes. She looked all around her, confirming that she was back home, and eventually she concluded that she was. She took stock of the situation, processing what they had told her. Ellie was satisfied that they had confirmed everything the Man had told her, they had made mistakes and were now trying to keep the worlds in balance with each other. The only thing she was unsure of was what she would be able to do to help. The first time she beat the Man she felt was more luck than skill, and the last time had been with the help of Emilia and using the energy. Maybe they were right, maybe she should practice. Ellie left the stones and headed home, she needed to get ready to visit Annabelle. As she walked, she was aware of everything around her, every plant, tree, bush, and animal. She could sense all of them moving as she passed by. This was enough to convince Ellie to try.

"I'm going to do this," she said to herself out loud as she walked. "I can practice, and I can beat him again and as many times as necessary."

It did not take her long to get home, she went upstairs and had a quick shower before getting changed. She was about to leave when she noticed a bag on the floor, tucked by the side of her drawers. Puzzled, she walked over and picked it up. Inside the bag was a photograph, a framed photograph of the Statue Of Mow. It was a gorgeous picture and Ellie immediately knew it was the one that Emilia had bought the day they had met. This brought a tear to her eye. She positioned the photo on top of her drawers and took a step back to see it properly.

"I'll do this for us, for Annabelle, Emilia, and I. I'm going to do this. I'm going to work at it, and I will be ready. If he comes back, I will be ready."

She smiled to herself, and left the house to go and meet

Annabelle, the love of her life.

The end of part two in The Book Of Imaginari.

ABOUT THE AUTHOR

Richard Hayden

At the time of writing The Book Of Imaginari (it began in 2019), Richard lived in the village of Mow Cop where it is set. He would often visit the folly and look out over the surrounding areas – it is this that led him to the inspiration for Imaginari.

Each part took around four months from concept to first draft, Part Three is coming soon.

The book was written for pleasure, creating it would fill his spare time and this opportunity was increased massively during the pandemic of 2020 – the goal being to create something that at least one person would find and enjoy reading it.

Let him know what you think of Imaginari, he can be contacted on Twitter and Instagram (@R_C_Hayden) and on Facebook (Richard Hayden Author, @rchaydenauthor), he would love to hear what you think of the story.

Printed in Great Britain
by Amazon